SGT GEORGE

THE RELUCTANT DETECTIVE

LEE HUGGETT

Edit and proof by

Gondor Writers Centre

www.gondorwriterscentre.com

SGT GEORGE

THE RELUCTANT DETECTIVE

LEE HUGGETT

www.facebook.com/leehuggettauthor
www.leehuggettauthor.com

First Published in 2022

© Copyright Lee Huggett 2022

The National Library of Australia Cataloguing-in-Publication

Creator: Huggett, Lee

Title: SGT George - The Reluctant Detective / Lee Huggett

ISBN: 978-0-6454997-0-4 (paperback)

Subjects: Fiction
Murder/mystery
Detective/crime
Dog fiction
Mental Health

Typeset in Times New Roman 12pt by Donna Munro Graphic Design.
Cover artwork by James Mossop and Donna Munro Graphic Design.
Printed and bound in Australia by Ingram Spark.

Acknowledgements

I would like to thank the first person brave enough to read my final manuscript: Jan. E. You pushed me to send it to an editor because you loved it and felt sure it would be a bestseller. It may well be gathering dust in a drawer still if it were not for your constant encouragement.

My Editor at the Gondor Writer's Centre: Thank-you for all your help and advice, and for having confidence in my ability to write and get this book published.

I also thank my other primary beta readers including those not mentioned in this cover: Julie Wahren who sat with me over many a wine after some killer nightshifts, as I pulled out my hair trying to decide on title names and the cover design. Cate Turner, for her enthusiasm, humour, and positive feedback. My old university friend, Claire Withers, who loved it too, but insisted I remove any stereotype negatives about bikers. I did. I also thank my family for their input and advice.

My primary cover designer James Mossop from the pinkoctopus.co.uk. who found exactly the right picture of George to go on the front cover. My secondary cover designer, Kozakura from Fiverr.com. I may use your design in the future.

I would also like to acknowledge all animals and humans who have suffered from the aftermath of war, both physically and mentally, as well as the thousands of mental health patients who have allowed me into their internal world.

I especially thank all animal refuges worldwide, including the Maryborough Dog Shelter in Queensland, Australia. Without those humans who are kind enough to volunteer their services to animals, I would not have my Penny or Zulu.

And last, but not least, I wish to thank and acknowledge every human being who is kind, loving and giving to all animals, be you vet, vegan or animal activist. To me, you are all true heroes.

Dedications

I dedicate this book to Penny (aka Charlie) and Zulu - my two doggy soulmates, whom I love dearly.

Truly, you are gifts from God.

Of course, I know how you would respond to that Penny. You'd snap back "If God was a Dog, there would be no doggy gifts to humans: For any sane, logical God would never have invented humans in the first place, let alone allow them to govern the Earth."

That is why I gave you a voice in this book Penny. A voice for all animals, all dogs, and yes, Zulu, cats too.

It is up to the reader to determine if you are right in your opinions, Penny.

I have made my decision.

You are. Xxx

Contents

Part One

Chapter 1

1800 hours

George was asleep when the first bomb exploded. When the second one hit, he was thrown against the wall of his flimsy shelter. As the ground beneath him began to tremble, the sandy walls around him threatened to collapse. When the bullets and missiles screamed past his shelter, he knew without doubt that his chances of survival were based on nothing more than luck.

And luck, of course, did not discriminate.

You could not rely on luck to save you, although there was always a chance that it would. In this situation, praying to luck was pointless, so George hunkered down and hoped for the best.

When another bomb exploded outside, he covered his ears from the deafening roar and watched the flickering lightshow through the thin veil of his tightly closed eyelids. As the blasts continued to gun their way through his veins, his heart thundered dangerously towards his throat and threatened to starve him of air. He gripped the shuddering earth and fought the urge to run, for to run would mean death, yet death was simply a hairsbreadth away. In such situations, he only had one option, so he took it. He took one large lungful of air, braced himself for impact and began to count.

On one, he felt his stomach do a double flip and he held in the urge to vomit.

At two, his head began to throb as another bomb screeched past his shelter.

By three, his brain was smashing away at the walls of his skull, like a maniac trying to escape a padded cell.

In a bid to control the madness, he adopted an age-old distraction technique: He began a debate, one born of logic that entailed the best options for death.

Before he hit five, he concluded that capture by the enemy was a far worse fate than death by incineration or suffocation beneath his shelter, so on five, he commenced his murder fantasy: A short visualisation of himself as he tore apart the enemy, piece by bitter piece, until on six, he felt triumphant, as their bloodied corpses lay beneath him.

When he hit seven, he blessed his comrades outside and prayed for their safety and at eight, he began to focus on dying. As he mentally urged his own death along, he imagined heaven, so that by the time he reached ten, he felt his mind unleash itself from his body and begin to float blissfully up into the sky.

At this point, he felt free from fear and pain, despite the fact that floating beside him were the arms and legs of his comrades and the sneering faces of the enemy.

Even though he was near to a state of loving forgiveness and total acceptance, he found he still took some bitter pleasure at the demise of his enemies. He noted with glee that those horrendous fluttery cloaks and dirt-white pyjamas were no longer attached to their bodies, and their bodies were no longer attached to their heads. As an added bonus, those dreadful beards were reduced to stubble, having been singed off by the searing heat of the flames.

However, his joy was short-lived.

By the time he hit eleven, the bombs had begun to recede into the distance. As the attack eased off, he was rudely jerked back into his body, which annoyed him greatly, for as expected, his bones were rattling, and his flesh felt like jelly.

When silence finally descended, he carefully inhaled a lungful of air. He had expected to be blasted with the usual stench of smoke and death, but instead he was met with the smell of fresh, fluffy carpets and furniture polish. As he shifted position, he felt the carpet beneath him and although he felt hot, he knew that he was pressed up against the central heater and not lying beneath a searing hot sun, surrounded by the dying flames of a thousand bombs. This meant that he was lying beneath the dining room table. It was a place he knew well, for he had often awoken beneath it imagining it was some kind of war shelter. Despite knowing this, he still refused to open his eyes and chose instead to home in on any sounds that might be suspicious.

Strangely, the only thing he could hear were the muted sounds of news reporters banging on about terrorism, covert operations, and bomb threats. The reporters, he realised, were simply spouting off from the TV by the sofa. The sofa that sat at the far end of the room, opposite the table.

With a sigh of relief, he opened his eyes. He was safe. He was not in Afghanistan. He was in drizzly old England, and for that, at least, he could finally thank luck.

Luck did discriminate.

It was luck that had saved him.

Or had it?

***

3

Before he could contemplate the implications of luck, he focused his mind on thoughts of England. As he visualised the cosy little village he lived in, with its historic buildings still intact and the lush green pastures which flanked its borders, he began to feel his beating heart still.

He listened to the sounds that drifted in through the open window. The sounds were barely audible: a few cars whizzing along the street outside; doors from nearby houses opening and closing; the movements of the neighbours on each side of the house as they watched endless soap operas or chatted about nothing. Superficial bullshit he called it. But pleasant, because one; it was superficial and two; most of it was bullshit.

He sniffed the air and knew it had been raining. Blissful rain, beautiful rain: cold, damp, and dark.

He felt reassured that roast dinners and Chinese take-aways were still on the menu and he felt glad that tonight was not Indian night, for those nights and those smells always reminded him of the turban and the terror. Indeed, he had been known to flip into a rage then spin into a nightmare simply because someone had walked past his house clutching a plastic bowl of tikka masala or beef vindaloo.

At times like that, he knew his grip on reality was tenuous at best. If the smell of vindaloo could spin him out, then what chance did he have if he walked outside and happened upon a man with a black beard? As he pondered this depressing thought, he recalled the sounds he heard before he drifted into his slumber. It was the sound of motorbikes. No wonder he had entered the terror.

The bikes were something he faced on a daily basis, for they belonged to a gang of hooligans over the road. The frequency in which they had invaded his life over the last six months meant he had become somewhat accustomed to them. But sometimes, without warning, the throaty growl of the engines and the oily stench of exhaust fumes would send him right back into the middle of a war zone. The noise of the bikes was nothing compared to the deafening scream of the bombs in 'Ghan, but when they triggered a nightmare, this gave him little relief.

It was no surprise then that he now found himself under the table, staring in terror at the flowery curtains that draped themselves over the big comfy sofa he'd been snoozing on when the bikes had roared past his house yet again.

He wished he could go outside and rip that gang to shreds. Their black leather jackets wouldn't last a second in his jaws. Even if he stood outside their house and barked until they went insane, that would give him some feeling of smug satisfaction. But going outside was not yet an option. A nightmare or flashback he could cope with, but the outside world he could not.

Apart from the motorbikes though, generally the neighbourhood was a peaceful place. Logically, he knew that. But when a nightmare or flashback occurred, he could not distinguish between his senses and reality.

Last night for example, he thought he heard a man running down the street yelling obscenities and screaming about terrorists. It had seemed so real, but he had concluded that it was simply another dream and had forced himself back into a blissful slumber.

This morning he had imagined that some kind of war battle was taking place outside his house. The noise of the screams had sent him ducking for cover, but this time he chose his safe place, the cupboard under the stairs. The cupboard was small, dark, and virtually soundproof. In that cupboard, he was sane. It was only the world outside that was mad. He could believe that. He could rest.

When his human arrived home that morning, she was in a foul mood. She had been working all night at the hospital, where she worked as a nurse. He noticed she was later than usual and for once, to his surprise, she did not criticise him for hiding out in his safe place. Instead, she downed a large vodka, then went to bed until early evening. When she awoke, she had raced back off to work again, but not before she had fed him his dinner and turned on the TV to keep him company.

George decided he would give the sofa another go. If he was interrupted again, he would sneak back into his cupboard. He heaved his hefty lump of a body off the carpet and plodded towards the sofa. He passed the TV, which was harking on about local threats and angry protesters. However, after this recent plunge into his own terror, he chose to remain oblivious to the news. As he hauled his hairy, brown hulk onto the sofa and drifted back into a deep, comforting slumber, he was going to wish he had paid more attention to that story: For it was that very event that would lead to a change in his dull, but gloriously peaceful existence, or at least, mostly peaceful. More peaceful than the war anyway.

Chapter 2

20.00 hours

Two hours later, George awoke with a jolt. His nose alerted him to something suspicious. A familiar smell drifted in through the open window behind him. It was the smell of dog.

Immediately he grew tense. The window looked out upon the back garden, but the back garden was fenced. Within a second, he regained his wits. Though it irked him to rise again from his slumber, he knew he would not relax.

Another sniff confirmed his suspicion, except this time he sensed more than one dog, yet not one human amongst them. He glanced at the front window and saw the moon grinning wildly, happy to celebrate its return from the dead.

George gripped the sofa with his meaty paws and forced himself to focus. He sensed trouble, and trouble was the last thing he needed. He carefully raised an eye, ear, and nose just above the sofa back. He needed to get some visual and auditory clarification. He prayed he was just being paranoid and hoped this was just

7

another dream. However, as his eye zoomed in towards the bushes, he knew he was awake and completely sane.

Two pairs of upright triangular ears poked up above the bushes defying gravity and homing in towards his house. A possible third pair of ears pushed the bushes to each side exposing what looked like a pair of furry mop heads. Although their bodies remained hidden, the light from the lounge reflected three sets of inquisitive eyes. They focussed intensely in his direction.

He hunkered down leaving an upright ear half hidden by the curtain. He thanked the breeze for blowing in his direction and hoped they had not seen his eye. They were whispering too. He could just make out the words. He pressed his ear nearer the window and heard one dog say, "Yes…this is the place. He lives almost opposite my house." It was a deep, gravelly voice, which was subdued by his attempt to talk quietly.

Then the doubtful voice of an older, male dog, "Yeah right, Sid. So how come he doesn't leave any wee mails at the lampposts for us? I've not seen him out and about round here. This can't be the place."

"He never goes for walks," replied Sid, "and he never comes out of his house. The only time he's been seen is when he's sitting in the car with his human."

"So, his human takes him for walks somewhere else then? Maybe they drive to the park?" the second male dog said.

"No. That's the strange part. They don't go anywhere. They just sit in the car in the driveway."

There was a pause before Sid continued, "It's really weird. I mean like seriously weird. His human practically drags him out of the house on a lead and then shoves him into the passenger seat. But what's really strange, is that she puts on a fake black beard and then wraps a tea towel on her head before she gets into the car beside him. She only does this when he's in the car though and she doesn't drive anywhere. She just sits there and revs up the engine."

There was a pause as the three dogs seemed to ponder this strange situation. George heard one of them choke down a snigger.

"What, so they don't go anywhere then? They just sit in the car?" This was the second male dog.

"Yep," replied Sid. "She keeps revving until he starts barking. Then she starts yelling at him to calm down. I'm telling you; we've all been watching through the windows. His human is as mad as he is."

The third dog spoke then. He spoke in high pitched youthful tones. "Yes, but Charlie said he's an ex-army war dog and that maybe he could help me."

This was followed by yet more sniggers.

"Yeah, right. How's he gonna help if he's too scared to come out? Check out the smell of his lawn for God's sake. The guy is completely petrified." This was Sid again.

"But Charlie said he's supposed to be a hero and that he's saved loads of lives. He must be brave. Plus, he's supposed to be really good at detecting and inspecting," said the young dog.

"Well, he obviously isn't very brave now, is he?" sneered the second dog. "Clearly this guy is a complete wimp."

"Well, I heard he was old, senile and about to cark it," said Sid haughtily. "I mean, why else would he stay indoors? He's big. I won't deny that, and he's got some weight on him, but it looks like fat to me. I don't reckon he could run a metre without gasping for breath. There's no point in asking him for help. Charlie's just trying to pacify you, Lad."

The young dog was not convinced. "But what if we bark and try to get him out here. Maybe if we tried…."

He was swiftly interrupted by Sid who said, "No. He's obviously useless now. Either that or all that heroic army talk is a pile of old codswallop. He's a coward, lad and we don't tolerate cowards in the dog world. We may as well forget it. Come on. Let's report back to Charlie."

There was a rustle of leaves as the three dogs quietly backed up through the bushes towards the fence and disappeared.

But to George, this made no sense. The fence had no gate, so where could they go?

Chapter 3

2020 hours.

George felt like a bomb had landed, right in the middle of his home! He sat on the couch for one minute, as if frozen in space, then he hurled himself off it and began to pace around the tiny lounge. He passed the TV again, which was now harping on about insurgents, but still he refused to listen. His mind was completely absorbed in this new turn of events.

Clearly, they knew about him then. If they knew, then who else knew? He felt his jaw throb with tension. He had been gritting his teeth throughout the whole sordid discussion.

So, they knew he was too scared to come out. Well of course he was scared. All those wide-open spaces and net-curtained windows? Who wouldn't be scared, especially if they knew what he knew? By God, the enemy could be hiding anywhere!

He realised it was ludicrous to compare a small English village such as Tichfield with the vast deserts and mountains of Afghanistan, but somehow, when he stepped outside, he was filled with surges of fear he could not control. These little sniggering snipers knew nothing of 'Ghan'. How they even knew he was an ex-army war dog perplexed him? The only way they could know was via his human. She had obviously been gossiping about him in a bid to explain her own odd behaviour.

He was annoyed with his human now. If she had spoken to the neighbours, then what else had she told them? He felt his ears burn with humiliation. He had been purposefully trying to keep a low profile and now it was obvious that the whole damn village knew his business, including those dogs.

He widened his pace until he was trotting angrily around the whole house. So, clearly, he was a complete laughingstock then? The brave war dog, who was too scared to come out and face a poncy, little English village?

He had no doubt that not one of those neighbours or their horrible little dogs had ever been to war. He had spent nearly his whole life in war zones: Eight long years serving Queen and country both in Iraq and Afghanistan. Eight years of searing heat sizzling his paws and dry desert sand up his nostrils. Eight years on covert patrol missions, dodging constant gun fire and enemy attacks.

Those dogs were pathetic. Useless brats. Whilst they were being pampered and petted, he'd been out there, sniffing out those bombs and killing the enemy. He'd saved hundreds of lives in the war, if not thousands. By God, he was an expert at bomb detection. The army had told him that. He had even been nicknamed 'Super-Nozer', because of his superior olfactory skills.

Those little whipper snappers knew nothing! They were little more than cuddly, teddy-bear pets with heart beats. What life had they seen? What danger had they ever faced? Indeed, had they ever worked for a living? The more he thought about it, the angrier he became. They had sneaked up and judged him with no damned knowledge of what he had been through.

As he contemplated their words, he began to fantasize about chasing them down and tearing them apart. Let them see what he was capable of. Let them see how fat, useless and senile he was! But then he realised that would be too easy. If he ripped them apart, it'd be quick, too quick. They deserved worse. Besides, his pride was at stake here and in order to recap it, he needed them to understand the war and how tough he really was.

As he worked himself up into yet more rage, he thought about the words he would sling at them instead. Let them hear about seeing his best mate Bill burn up in flames before him, or Johnny's tail come flying off his body when he stepped on a mine. Let them hear of the blood, torture, and carnage he had faced. Of the throats he had torn apart in a bid to save the soldiers. Let them hear about Sadie.

It was then that he stopped pacing. At the mere thought of Sadie, his heart tore into a thousand pieces. He hurled himself back onto the sofa and curled up into a tight little ball.

Sadie.

He felt his rage disintegrate and, in the distance, he heard a muffled howl. He realised it was he who was howling. Howling at the injustice of it all. Howling at how it had all ended: for him and for her. He heard himself whine as he recalled their last patrol. The patrol that had led to his downfall. The patrol where he had lost both his spirit and his beloved friend.

His mind lurched to one side as he envisioned the scene. He and Sadie had been stationed at Pajaki in Afghanistan. He was based with the Brits, whilst she had arrived with the US Army. Sadie was an American Alsatian with silver hair and glacier blue eyes. George had never met a dog with blue eyes. Immediately, he had been struck by her beauty. It was her character that he grew to

13

love though. As tough and determined as any other war dog, she still retained a soft and vulnerable side. It was a trait he was rarely privy to, for most war soldiers, both human and dog, chose to hide such traits under a hardened exterior.

Over a period of six months, he had formed a deep and loving friendship with Sadie. It had been her first posting following her basic training, so she had been nervous and shocked by the events in the war. Although she had her own human dog trainer, George enabled her to sharpen her skills in both bomb detection and covert attack operations.

When the soldiers had been caught and held hostage, he had shown her how to maintain a low profile until it was safe to attack the enemy and free their comrades. He had coached her through the trauma of seeing the soldiers lose their lives and helped her adjust to the noise and the harsh conditions they faced each day.

As her knowledge increased, so did her confidence. She had an infectious sense of humour, which George knew was her way of dealing with the atrocities they witnessed each day.

However, she had also developed a sense of the invincible and he had warned her that such a trait could be dangerous and could easily lead to serious mistakes. When he told her this she had laughed and told him not to be such a 'silly old bore'. George fretted though. He had lost too many war friends through carelessness. Confidence like this, was merely a mask for a soldier's underlying fear, and actions motivated by fear were not reliable.

During their time together, their base in Pajaki had been in the early stages of development. The base was extremely vulnerable due to its isolation in the vast desert mountains of Afghanistan. The Army had been finding it impossible to build due to a constant barrage of nightly mortar attacks from the Taliban. The soldiers decided that they had no option but to eliminate the problem.

That night, an American and British patrol team had headed out on a long and windy mountain road. Their mission was to locate the caves where it was suspected the mortars were being stored and launched. Their plan was to capture the enemy and their cache of weapons, and hence reduce any further attacks on the base.

As per plan, George and Sadie were to lead the way. They were both competent enough to work off leash, but their dog handlers were not far behind. Their initial task was to ensure that the patrol was forewarned of any impending danger. The insurgents could attack from any direction at any time but both Sadie and he would sniff them out in an instant. Sadie trotted beside him, at a distance of 20 metres. As they neared the caves, they slowed the pace, crouched down low and moved in silently.

It was Sadie who discovered the bomb first – buried in the sand. She gave her warning signal, and the patrol commander gave the order for Sadie's dog handler, Corporal Jones, to go in and investigate. Unfortunately, unbeknown to Sadie, that particular bomb had a sensitive and complex trigger mechanism. Backing off immediately and circumnavigating the bomb was what was really required. Instead, Sadie in her innocence stepped forward and tripped the mechanism.

George was the only one who heard the trigger click, but by then it was too late. Within a split second he was flung to one side as the bomb exploded. The sound of the bomb had screamed through his ears and the heat from the flames chased his racing body. The patrol retreated and immediately fired their guns towards the caves.

For George though, it was over. Sadie was dead. He recalled how he had fled from the scene: fled as far as his legs could take him, until he fell in an exhausted heap in the rubble of dirt on the frozen sand. As the bombs exploded and the guns fired around him, all he could think of was his beloved Sadie. The only true friend he had ever had in this terrible war. Now she'd been burned to a cinder. She was nothing more than the dust that drifted around him in the desert breeze. The hole in his heart gaped open, and yet again, loneliness crept in to fill the gap where Sadie's love had once resided.

If it had been him who had discovered the bomb, he would have known instantly to avoid it. He felt torn with guilt. He had taught her about many bombs, but he had not yet informed her about that one. Even before she had given her warning signal, he had recognised the stench of that bomb. But the Patrol Commander had acted too swiftly. Before George could react, Corporal Jones had already covered half the distance between the team and Sadie.

As George lay in the dust, he howled for her broken body: for her beautiful eyes, her fun-loving nature, and the bravery in her huge, soft heart. He wept and howled for all his friends, both dog and human alike, who had died in that war or who had gone home missing some essential part of their being.

For George, that posting had been his last. He had dedicated his whole life to the army. He had been a proud and loyal soldier. But after that, after Sadie, he no longer saw the value in either his role or the war.

Instead, fear and hatred consumed him. He despised the Taliban now. It seemed that wherever he turned, there was yet another man standing there with a big black beard and a gun hidden under his cloak. They were relentless. An enemy that seemed to get larger by the day despite the army's efforts to blow up every town and village under suspicion.

He realised then that the war would never end. He was exhausted, and his existence seemed as bleak and as pointless as the white desert sand that stretched endlessly before him day after day and year after year.

After that incident, he became volatile. The mere sight of a black beard, fluttery cloak or headscarf would either send him into an uncontrollable rage or see him diving for cover under the nearest bush.

He rarely slept and instead paced anxiously around the compound all night. He felt constantly on alert and the slightest sound would set him on edge. A gentle rustle of leaves from a nearby bush or the soft tread of boots would immediately send him into a state of panic. Everything became suspicious. Rousing his comrades from their much-needed sleep and sending them ducking for cover from a potential bomb threat or crouching low with guns at the ready became an all too frequent event.

But more often than not, he was wrong. He was exhausting the troops. Too often they found themselves lying low and pointing their guns in the direction George had indicated, only to find that it was Sergeant Biggs or Private Smith taking a leak behind a dusty dune. Other nights, they would be sleeping through the background sounds of enemy fire when suddenly George would leap on their beds and seek refuge beneath their sleeping bags.

As his anxiety increased and his concentration diminished, his detecting and investigating skills were becoming unreliable and costly. If the troops went out on a covert operation, he found he was frequently being left behind to 'guard the camp'.

Finally, the army decided to suspend him from duty. They called it "early retirement" and tactfully informed him it was time he was sent home to live a life of leisure and one, they strongly insisted, he deserved. They thanked him for the eight years he had served both Queen and country and reminded him of the numerous medals he'd been awarded for his bravery and the countless lives he had saved. They told him that despite the fact he had killed the enemy in combat, seen his comrades blown to pieces, burnt to death, or disabled, he had never once swayed from his duty or allowed his skills to be compromised.

Indeed, they continued kindly, he had been regarded as "one of their best" and there was no doubt that his detecting and investigating skills were more than merely superior.

Of course, the soldiers knew that George had never recovered after Sadie. They had watched him slowly disintegrate. They had laid stiffly awake on their beds as he had howled on and on at the moon outside, as if somehow, by howling, he could bring her back or join her. It had broken their hearts. They too, had been affected by Sadie's loss. No one wanted to see a dog get killed. No one wanted to see a dog become mentally unwell due to the loss of another dog. George was one of the longest serving dogs in the army and he had not even chosen the job. It was a stab in the guts for them all.

On his final day, the Brits awarded George the Dickin Medal. It was the highest award for British Military Dogs. Then, as a special exception, in the same momentous ceremony, the US Army awarded Sadie a Purple Heart. It was an American medal given to wounded or dead soldiers and not usually dogs. So, for the US Army, it was a major event: A medal given to those who had shown exceptional bravery, nobility, and sacrifice. With a grand gesture, that only the Americans can pull off, they put Sadie's Purple Heart on George. Sadie was dead and belonged to the US Army. There was no one else to receive her Purple Heart and no one, the Army insisted, deserved it more than George.

George's heart was broken. Although he wore the medal, it was with some bitterness and a great deal of pain. He knew he looked a mess. His shoulders sank, his ears flopped down, and he spent most of the ceremony staring at the floor. He felt no sense of pride. Just guilt, confusion, and grief. Before the Army could witness him howl with anguish again, they had shoved him into the army car and with a great cheer, had waved goodbye to their hero. They told him he would love England, and he would love the new human they had chosen for his companion.

When he left his comrades, he was wearing her heart and when the plane took off, screaming like a missile, no one heard him howl. He had lost his love, his job, and his mind. All he had ever known was the war. Now he had this thing called retirement to tackle. It sounded incredibly boring. He had not wanted to leave Afghanistan. For him, it had meant leaving Sadie. He had hoped they would put him out of his misery, like they did to many war dogs who had served their time.

When that never happened, he had even contemplated intentionally stepping on a bomb. Anything to be away from his pain and back with Sadie again. But who knew what lay on the other side of this life? If he took his own, then he might not see her.

So yet again, like any good soldier dog, he was told what to do and he blindly obeyed.

***

As George uncurled himself from his tight little ball on the sofa, he recalled the moment he had landed in England. As the army car had driven him through the quaint little village he now lived in, *Tichfield they called it,* he had felt a huge burden lift from his shoulders. He still felt anxious though. He noted that people lived in houses behind net curtains, and he felt suspicious. What had they to hide that they needed curtains? It was undoubtedly safer than The Ghan, but he decided he would reserve his judgment until he felt assured that the place was safe.

When he met his new human, he felt instantly relieved. She was young, kind but assertive. He discovered she was an ex-army nurse and a dog handler. At the time, he had recalled feeling pleased about this. He was not so sure now. That had been six months ago, in the spring, when the smell of daffodils had drifted in through the army car window and he had felt some small measure of hope. Hope that he could at last relax. Hope that he could eat and sleep, without need or worry, without having his nerves frayed by constant attacks by the enemy.

Unfortunately, George's hopes were soon dashed. He discovered that his human had developed an interest in psychology; an obsession he found morbid. He had done his time with psychopaths and unlike his human, he had no desire to re-hash it all in some last-ditch attempt to understand, justify or rectify it. He knew he had been affected by the war and he knew why. The baddies attacked the goodies and the goodies attacked back and then got damaged. Why she had to question that was beyond him.

However, he had little time to ponder her logic. He had barely gotten his paws on the mat before she had diagnosed him with Post Traumatic Stress Disorder.

Within weeks, he found that his every move was scrutinised, analysed, and then treated accordingly. If he flattened his ears he was 'anxious'. If he slept for too long, he was 'depressed'. If she witnessed him rolling about in his sleep, she would rise him from his slumber and reassure him that he was just experiencing a nightmare.

There was little doubt that she was right in her diagnosis. He was a mess. He refused to leave the house except to use the back garden for his toilet. But apart from the times when his human went to work, he found that the chances of him zoning out on the sofa and waiting for a welcome death were zero.

His human was determined to 'cure' him and he was soon exposed to another training regime, which he found more bewildering and anxiety provoking than the basic training he had completed prior to the war.

She called this training Behavioural Therapy and told him that in time, with 'graduated exposure', she would extinguish his fears. He soon learnt what all this meant. It became quite normal for him to doze off on the sofa only to be awoken by a thunderous clap followed by her jumping out in-front of him donning a fake black beard and a bath towel on her head. The clap, she told him, was to get him used to sounds resembling war weapons – like roaring motorbikes and noisy car engines – while the beard and head towel were to reduce his fear of potential Taliban look-a-likes.

He hated that fake black beard. Just seeing it would send a cold shiver up his spine. Yet his human was adamant that exposure to the beard would cure him, especially if it was placed near something nice. Recently, she had taken to wearing it when she fed him his dinner. It made him want to vomit and he spent many an hour in fantasy-land daydreaming about ripping it to shreds. But each time he got near it, when she left it on the floor near his dinner bowl for example, he had frozen in fear.

Once he did destroy it, but it had cost him a panic attack and two days recovering in his safe place under the stairs. It had made no difference. His human had said that mastery over the beard meant he was progressing, so she purchased another beard, plus a few spares.

When he tried to hide his anxiety, in the hope that she would consider him cured, she had told him that his increasing acceptance of these 'treatments' was 're-assuring'. This meant that he could 'graduate' outside to the car. It was a thought that terrified him, but she insisted that it was a necessary procedure if he were to obtain that allusive thing called peace and happiness.

In time, he became convinced that it was her happiness that was at stake. Her increasing alcoholic binges and time off sick from work, were evidence to him that she was as much of a nervous wreck as he was. It pained him to see her crying out in terror as she rolled about in her nightmarish world. It took little effort on his part to imagine what she was seeing.

He noted too that she had few, if any, real friends. Indeed, he knew, without doubt, that he was her only friend. As the months progressed, he grew to love her as much as the comrades he had loved and lost in the war.

However, her relentless psychological strategies were becoming tiresome and irritating. He realised that he was not interested in happiness. His greatest desire in life was to eat and sleep as much as possible. He did not want to face life, for by then it was all too daunting. He was emotionally exhausted, and her physical affections and pampering were what he sought more than anything.

He knew he was anti-social and agoraphobic, so her attempts at getting him outside for a walk were fruitless. He had sat in the car a few times but that was as far as he was prepared to go. He knew he was a hopeless case. He had gone insane, and he knew it. Going outside terrified him and he hated himself for the wreck he'd become. Yet despite feeling ashamed of himself, he knew that part of him no longer cared. All he wanted now was to numb his emotions and forget the war. Forget everything, except his beautiful friend Sadie.

These dogs though? They put a whole new perspective on things. As he lay slumped on the sofa, their conversation broke into his thoughts. They had implied he was weak, useless, and fat. The little rotters knew nothing of his life. They knew nothing of real life! He felt his jaw tighten in anger and once again he found himself pacing around the lounge in ever widening circles. When he could bear it no longer, he raced up and down the stairs until he was gasping for breath.

22

As his anger turned to rage, he could hear that familiar clicking sound again. The same click he had heard before Sadie's demise. His brain began to feel like a ticking time-bomb ready to explode and he felt an urgent need to break loose from this tiny house. It was restricting his movements and his sudden need to expel his energy in a violent manner.

He began to rationalize his next move. His human companion had gone to work. She would be out for the night. If he went out now, she wouldn't notice. Again, he thought about the words he could hurl at those dogs. The dogs' comments had cut right into the core of his tough army ego. He wanted to watch them sweat and grovel. To let the weight of guilt squash down their egos, then torture them slowly so they could experience every single hurt and injury his war friends had suffered. He wanted them to experience fear. Feel the fear he had experienced all his life.

As he considered their fate, his mind began to clear. He considered the young dog. For some reason he didn't think he deserved to be punished. The lad had wanted his help and had sounded quite desperate.

In fact, the more he thought about it the more he realised that it was really the young lad who wanted him out. This aroused his curiosity and fed into his long-forgotten sense of importance. However, the other two had simply dismissed him.

He felt his hatred intensify and again he imagined ripping them apart. He would enjoy it too. He was sick of suppressing his anger. Taking it out on them would be a healthy release, he reasoned. Better than any of these so-called therapies he had to suffer. If he showed them who was boss, then maybe he could rectify the appalling rumours about him. Perhaps then the village would start to talk about him as a hero and not some snivelling coward hiding out behind fluttery curtains.

He decided at once that this was exactly what he would do. Tear them to pieces, but only after he had let them know what it meant to be in the army. Tell them all the horrific details and then see if they too thought they could come home in one sodden piece. The only trouble was, that would mean he would have to venture outside and find them. He would be alone, in the dark and without any comrades or combat gear. As these conflicting thoughts surged around his brain, he knew he needed to do something.

The army had told him three things: Follow your gut instinct, ignore your fear, and take immediate action.

Though he hated to admit it, his gut instinct told him he had everything to lose and nothing to gain if he did not go out right now and face those little bastards.

Chapter 4

20.45 hours

George raced immediately to the back door. He was fully intent on storming outside to investigate those bushes. Instead, he braked hard, slid on his haunches, and now found himself peering cautiously at the dog flap, completely immobilised by fear.

He slammed his tail down on the floor in frustration. *Damn this anxiety.* His mind had taken over too quickly. Instead of taking action, his imagination was now embroiled in a seething mass of frightening scenarios. What if he located the dogs and they were more vicious than he had originally thought? What if he confronted them and then froze in fear? What if he stuttered and couldn't get his words out? If he panicked and showed any signs of anxiety, he would be a laughingstock. Already he had been the butt of their jokes and he had no desire to confirm their theories about him being weak and useless. The temptation to return to his warm, comfy sofa intensified. Maybe he should give it a miss. Go out tomorrow instead.

Again, he remembered his army training. Don't think, just do it! If he didn't go now, he knew he never would. Then he really would feel a failure. Besides, he still felt curious. These dogs had sought him out. They had wanted to utilise his investigating skills for a reason.

He recalled the value the army had placed on his nose. There had been much talk of modelling a virtual nose on his at one point. Such an invention would have saved hundreds of war dog lives. He had to remember these things, including his bravery. Few people had survived his physical assaults and lived to tell the tale, unless of course he had wanted them to.

If these measly little fur pets thought they could take him on in physical combat, they would be eaten alive! As these thoughts surged around his brain, he knew he could not turn back.

The dog flap glared back at him. It stood tall and square, like a commanding officer urging him on. Somewhere in the back of his mind he heard the encouraging words of Sadie, "Come on, George. Let's do it. The enemy can't beat us!"

Before he could contemplate these words further – the last ones Sadie had ever spoken – and before he could feel that familiar stab of pain in his heart, he leaned back, braced himself for impact and flew out the dog flap with a resounding crash.

***

George was flying: Like a bold army jet streaking across the cold dark sky, his quivering heart became a distant memory. Instead, it roared, like the powerful engine driving the jet. As his huge brown paws touched down upon the soft, damp lawn, he felt a charge of adrenaline course through his body.

Within a split second he felt himself change. Before he could consider this, he did a double forward roll followed by a single side roll and landed stock still, in a crouching stance, in front of the bushes. His breath slowed into a gentle rhythm and his ears stood alert, rotating on his head like a pair of triangular satellites. A world of scents assaulted his nose, a nose that immediately set about its natural task of dissecting and analysing each smell until there was nothing left to comprehend.

He remained in this position for a full two minutes, absorbing every piece of information he senses could detect. It was as if he had just come alive and had landed himself right in the middle of a war zone. He could hear every sound in the minutest detail, right down to the gentle whisper of the bushy leaves, to the insects marching their way across the lawn and the worms shuffling around in the mud under his paws. Far off in the distance, he heard the bustling sounds of cars racing along the highway. Nearby, he heard the neighbours in their homes talking above the drone of the television as their dinner plates crashed around in the kitchen sinks.

By the third minute, George realised how utterly dead he had been just minutes before. He had been so engrossed in mindless, endless worries, so tense with fear and anger or dulled by sleep and food, he had forgotten how extraordinary life and the planet around him was. He had been waiting for death, yet all along, he had already been dead.

At this point all fear completely dissipated. He felt focused, alert, and alive. He recalled his mission – to locate and eliminate those dogs – and he immediately set about the task of sniffing them out.

With his newfound confidence, George sauntered into the bushes and readied his nose for action. Immediately, he got a whiff of where the dogs had been hiding. Standing in their spot, he glanced back at the house and saw the window he had been peering through whilst they had gossiped about his heroic demise.

27

He sniffed again. So, they had been cautious. Not a drop of urine had been left upon the patch where they had stood. However, their paw prints were clearly visible. Three sets. Twelve prints. He sniffed each one and observed the size. The paws were tiny, barely a quarter the size of his. This seemed strange. Their ears had been huge? He had expected them to be larger. Now he realised they were dwarves. Nothing more than mini monstrosities.

Reassured by this, he sniffed his way to the back fence. It was an old wooden fence and he noticed that one of the posts had been pushed to one side. It left a gap in the fence just big enough for three small dogs to sneak through. He nudged at the other fence posts, but they remained solidly fixed in their position.

The gap was not big enough for him to crawl through and he cursed silently. He carefully poked his nose through the gap to survey the scene behind the fence. When he did, he was surprised. Stretched before him lay a large woody parkland. He hadn't realised that before. Usually, he raced into the back garden, did his business in a blind panic, and then dashed back indoors to recover from the trauma of being outside. Now he realised that his back garden stood amongst a row of others, which all backed onto this park.

As he continued to look, he noticed that it was rectangular in shape with a row of houses flanking the opposing side. These too were hidden by walls or fence lines. The park was about 700 metres in length and ended each side at a road. The houses across from him were approximately 200 metres away. Within this park were an array of bushes and trees. A perfect haven for animal dens and doggie hideouts.

So far George knew of three dogs, but he knew there was at least one more – the fellow called Charlie who had not been with this little pack of miniatures. He knew not the size of Charlie, but he guessed that he was the pack leader.

If this Charlie was big and there were yet larger dogs in the pack, he realised he would have to remain vigilant. Compared to Afghanistan, this park would be easy to navigate. However, he was up against a different enemy now: one that had the same skills as he in sensory detection. Humans were easy to sneak up on and attack. They had poor olfactory and auditory skills. These dogs could pose a problem if they too were vigilant. Conversely, as they were pets, he doubted they could outsmart him.

He listened carefully. Although he could hear an array of nightly sounds, he could not hear the dogs nor yet sniff their presence. He would have to get out there but how? He cursed the fact that he had eaten so much food and gained weight. But he knew he would never have been able to squeeze through the fence gap. He decided that the only way out was under. He focused his efforts and began to dig.

Within five minutes he had created a tunnel big enough for him to crawl through and he soon found himself peering over the edge. With one last squeeze and a quick check to ensure he remained unobserved, he crawled out of the tunnel and followed the paw prints to the first set of bushes five metres away.

As he drew near, his nose immediately alerted him to the smell of dog urine. One quick sniff and he knew they had been both scared and excited. He detected the young lad's urine and realised he was barely into his teen years. Although he was healthy and fit, something bothered him. It was more than anxiety. He seemed tormented by a range of emotions including anger, terror, heartbreak, and distress. There was a sense of hopelessness too in his little puddle of urine, and for some reason, this saddened George. He tried to ascertain the dogs' ancestry, but this was impossible. The lad was a combination of so many dog breeds that it boggled his mind.

George was a pedigree. He was a German Shepherd and built perfectly for war. He briefly wondered if mixing up breeds like this led to psychological disorders and then cursed himself for adopting his humans' theories and pathologizing normal behaviours. No. This dog had a reason to be upset and it had nothing to do with being of mixed breed.

He moved on to the other two patches of urine. From these, he detected that both were male, and both were aggressive and selfish. He recognised the breed of one dog – a Jack Russell. This explained the dog's aggression and the large difference in his ear to paw ratio.

The other dog was a mystery though. His smell suggested one of those small, white fluffy dogs that were often adopted as pet army mascots. He had never learned their breed, yet they were usually quite loveable in a cutesy type of way, which is why they made good pets. Yet the smell of urine from this dog seemed at odds with this type of dog. His personality was too offensive. It made George feel uneasy, enough so that he suddenly felt as if he were being watched – as if a bearded man with a Turban was hiding out amongst the trees and aiming his gun straight at his ears.

He decided that the urine probably belonged to Sid. He'd not yet met Sid, but he already hated him. He had been hiding out in the bushes in his garden after all, and the way in which he had slated George's character seemed not that much different from having the barrel of a gun pointed at his face. The Taliban had wanted to destroy George physically, for he was a threat to their attack strategies. Sid however, had attempted to decimate his character, and somehow, after all he had been through, this seemed worse than a bullet.

Yet it also suggested that Sid felt threatened by George and knowing that, knowing that the dog might be quite wary of him, gave him a sudden burst of confidence. Sid and the others were miniatures after all. If they annoyed him, he'd just tear them apart. How hard could it be? He decided to follow their trail.

He had only walked a few more metres before he picked up their scent. It took him a minute to discover their den. It was a mere one hundred metres from where he stood. As he drew closer, he could hear them chatting. He ensured he was downwind of them and approached the den, lying low and remaining well-hidden.

Through a small opening in a clump of bushes, he could see the outline of their body shapes in the moonlight. There were four dogs in total. Four mini-monsters. Three of the dogs were laying on their stomachs, head on paws, whilst the fourth dog sat by the entrance of the den. The three dogs who lay together did not seem particularly anxious about being seen. In fact, they seemed rather relaxed considering they were in a big, open parkland.

If this was the case, then maybe they were protected by larger pack members hiding in other locations. He felt uncomfortable not having anyone cover his back, but he hunkered down in a bush to watch and listen.

Only one dog looked anxious – the young one. Although he sat by the entrance, he did not appear to be absorbed in the task of guard duties. Instead, he gave off an aura of one whom did not fit in, an outsider who sat near the pack yet did not belong. His attention seemed directed elsewhere, away from these dogs. He sat very still, and his thin, little tail curled protectively around his body. He stared absently into the distance, yet though alert, his shoulders sank down, as if a great, big, sledgehammer had driven its way into the depths of his soul.

The other dogs were clearly unperturbed by the misery of one of their pack.

"I don't get it," said one, and George immediately realised it was the tiny Jack Russell. "Why do they bother changing their fur for every occasion? They've got furs for walking, furs for shopping, furs for work and fur for bed. Then they have to wash them all and then wash themselves. We've got one set of fur and it serves every purpose."

"Yeah, and then they wash hundreds of pots and plates after every meal. We just have one bowl. Humans are always moaning about all that work but if they did less washing, they'd have more time to play. They really are stupid." This was the voice of Sid, a deep gravelly voice that George immediately recognised.

"Humans are illogical, Sid. They swan about like they own the place and destroy everything in their way. They're a disabled, dependent, and selfish species. I don't particularly like them that much, but I suppose there are a few good ones around." This was the voice of a female. She was a small dog, yet her voice cut through the air like broken glass.

The Jack Russell continued, "What I don't get is the whole sitting business. Why is it that we have to sit down all the time, even before we are about to eat? I mean, I don't sit down when I eat my food. Humans do but they're different. Why do they expect us to do the same?"

The female spoke again, in clipped tones which seemed at odds with her relaxed demeanour. "It's all about authority. They want to dominate us. Make sure that we know that they have control."

George noticed her back stiffen.

"Humans seem obsessed with power," she continued, "It's utterly ridiculous. I think they're scared we might try and overthrow them, which we could and probably should, but what's the point when we get free food. However, as far as I'm concerned, they only ever got their power because of us." With that said, she sat up and slammed her tail onto the ground.

George noticed a change in her voice and even from this distance he could sniff the anger exuding from her fur. As he listened, he was surprised at her level of knowledge.

"For example," she said, "did you know that many years ago humans were running around like us in the wild? According to my mother they were useless animals. Weak defenceless beings of the lowest order. It wasn't until they made tools, weapons, and fire that they became what they are today. But apparently that was only because they used us. I mean think about it," she continued in full swing, as again she slammed her tail down, "Human animals are pathetically weak. They have no decent jaws or claws to tear apart their prey, they've no sense of smell, a pair of useless ears, they can't see in the dark and they've no fur to keep themselves warm.

"If we set about hunting them down, they'd be easy to catch. Not only that, they've got two ridiculously weak legs, so they can't run fast and they've no wings to make up for the fact. It's unbelievable," she said as she now got up and began to pace around the tiny den. "Humans used to hang around us like vultures waiting for us to make a kill so they could eat our leftovers."

As her pace grew faster her voice took on a more venomous tone. "The bones they sling at us today and all the crummy leftovers we get were once thrown at them from us! Now, it's the other way around. The only reason they got where they are today was because of us dogs!

"According to my mother, they abducted our puppies and raised them to do all the hunting and guard duties. Then, when they had all that sorted, and the best portions of meat as well, they had plenty of time to think about other methods of killing and developing themselves and thus developed what we know today as human tools, weapons, and fire! I tell you all," she said, wagging her tail in a frenzy, "humans strut around as if they're top dog and they treat us like scum, but in truth they should be worshiping us and holding us in the highest esteem. But do you know what story they tell each other instead? Do you?"

By now, her jaws were almost snapping at the faces of the two small dogs. To George, it seemed as if she were about to rip them to shreds.

As Sid and the Jack scratched awkwardly at various bits of their body and silently nodded their agreement with her, she yelled, "They say that we... we... a species that can survive in the wild with no need for weapons, clothes, or fire, actually approached them first and begged for their leftover food! I mean, seriously? How friggin stupid is that!"

At that she sat down and sighed. George could see that she was exhausted with her rant, and he noted the other two dogs gave out a quiet sigh of relief themselves.

"Well," she said, her tone now more sedate, "I suppose they do hold us in high esteem by keeping us as pets and that's probably why they can't let us go. They know damn well, deep inside, that if it wasn't for us, they'd have died out eons ago. They've copied our identity, believe they are top of the food chain, but ultimately, they are nothing more than scavengers. This stupid idea that they are the superior species and top of the food chain, has completely ruined the natural balance of our Earth." She settled back down with her head in her paws. "It's just a shame most dogs have forgotten their true purpose. Instead, they chase a ball and run around like idiots entertaining humans. Now, all dogs are entirely dependent on them. It's utterly pathetic."

The two male dogs chuckled as if agreeing with the female, but after a pause, Sid asked her, in almost careful tones, if she loved her humans.

"I have no idea what you mean by love, Sid," replied the female. "I mean, I like my current humans and certainly I would protect them. They have been kind to me after-all. But mostly I don't trust humans. They can be moody, unpredictable, and selfish. They make everything complicated, and I would much

34

prefer a dog as my friend than a human. At least I know where I stand!"

As Sid grunted in agreement with this comment the young dog raised his ears in anger and joined in on the conversation. "That's true. The humans hate me, and they hate my human. It's not fair!"

Despite this sudden emotional outburst from the lad, the other dogs remained slumped on their stomachs and continued to moan on about their humans. It was almost as if the lad had not spoken.

"It's so true," said the tiny Jack Russell as he now got up and began to wag his tail in a frenzy. "I mean humans can't even wipe their own arse without using a ton of loo roll and what other animal, bird or fish has to use loo roll or even a leaf to wipe their bums? They're so stupid."

The loo roll topic seemed to break the tension and the three dogs fell about laughing. George had to agree with them, indeed he had never considered the issue of loo roll before, and although the scene had been rather tense, he had to agree with much of what these hateful little dogs had said. In fact, he had found it quite intriguing. Most of his life he had been bossed around in the army. He had assumed he was a simple, albeit brave, but subservient soldier.

However, now he thought about it, it was the army who had relied on him, because it was the army, the humans, who were ill equipped to do his job. A job they had not even invented a machine to do yet.

He was keen to hear more, but suddenly he noticed the young lad stiffen. The lad remained at the entrance, with his back to the others, glaring into space. George could sniff the anger exuding from his fur, yet to George, he sensed this had little to do with the topics in question. Yet again, the other three dogs ignored this obvious signal.

"That's so true about the bog roll," chuckled Sid, thrashing his tail from side to side. "It's so typical of humans. I mean, what are they gonna do when they run out of loo roll? They're utterly ridiculous. Why can't they just adapt their bodies to the natural world like us? Why can't they simply evolve with nature instead of fighting it?"

"Yes, but they will lose in the end, Sid," snarled the female, who had rapidly lost her sense of humour. "Their greed and insanity, their selfish disregard for the natural earth and all the animals will ultimately see their demise, and by Dogs' God I shall be there watching them rot!" As the hatred leached out from her fur, the two male dogs glanced at each other. Even from this distance, George could see they looked uncomfortable.

"I tell you what," said the Jack Russel suddenly, "Why don't we play 'what-did-your-human-do-today?'" At this Sid and the female chortled and rapidly wagged their tails in agreement.

"Okay. Well, I'll start." The Jack sat up, cleared his throat, and expanded his tiny chest as if he were about to make an important announcement. "Today, my humans decided they were going camping next week. They said they wanted to escape from their complex lives and experience a more natural life in the wild." The Jack chuckled. "Well anyway, they decided to make a list of camping stuff to take. Oh my God! You should have heard the list. Tents, sleeping bags, pots, pans, cooker, plates, cups, knives, forks, tins of beans, furs for bed and furs to keep warm, coolie boxes, fishing rods. You wouldn't believe it," he said as he flapped his tail from side to side, "I pretty much thought they were simply moving house. I mean how did they ever survive in the wild without all that stuff? What other animal needs any stuff apart from the fur on their backs?"

As the Jack ranted on about how stupid his humans were, and his tail wagged ever faster, the other two dogs fell onto their backs and snorted and chuckled in union.

As the chuckles grew into outright hysterical laughter, the young lad turned to glare at them. George couldn't see the lad's eyes, but he could read the body language. The lad was fuming.

"Okay," he suddenly yelled, "How about this then. Today, my human was wrongly accused of murder and then rudely arrested and thrown into jail, which means now, I haven't got a human!" He slammed his bony tail on the ground and turned back to stare into the night.

When George heard this, he was quite horrified. No wonder the lad was disturbed. Clearly, he had experienced a traumatic experience and was now homeless as well. He looked at the other dogs and immediately felt disgusted by their apparent disregard for the lads' plight. His plea was dramatic and shocking, yet the three dogs continued to ignore him. The lad was clearly in need of help, yet this lot seemed not to care. Although he had to agree with much of what they said, their contempt for their humans was pointless, especially if they ran back to their cosy little homes and ate the human trash they moaned about.

They reminded him of a bunch of drunken officers in the higher echelons of the army. A ruthless lot who'd bark out orders to the soldiers, then sit around drinking themselves stupid as their human comrades got blown to bits. The lad was clearly nothing more than cannon fodder to them. Irrelevant and expendable.

More significantly, George thought, and given recent events, he had expected that he would be the central theme in their conversation. Obviously, they had already written him off! He decided that as he was now so unimportant to them, and after all he had been through to get there as well, it was time to execute plan A: March right on in there, assert his authority, and demand their attention!

However, before he could move, he heard the young lad pipe up again. "Why are you all acting so casual? My life is still at risk here and we haven't done anything. We should be looking for that cat. We should have barked and woken up that Inspector!"

Sid replied, but to George's annoyance, the dog didn't even bother to sit up. "What's the point? He's obviously a loser. Just forget it, lad."

George snarled, but before he could gather his wits and stand up, the young lad yelled, "Well I don't care what you lot think. He's my only hope and I am getting him out here right now!"

There was a sudden breeze as the dog leapt onto his paws and flew past George at a speed he had never witnessed before in his whole entire army career. Before he had time to even consider this unexpected event, the lad had raced towards his house, picked up his scent, and back-tracked immediately. With a warning bark, he now stood two metres behind him. By the time George had lifted his nose off the ground, four pairs of eyes glared down at him, like vicious little vultures surrounding their prey.

Chapter 5

2130 hours

George was mortified. They had caught him out like a sneaky little spy! He looked nothing like the commanding presence he had envisaged he would be.

He realised he had to act swiftly. To delay now would be the death of his ego. Without pause for further thought, he jumped up onto his meaty paws, raised his tail like a baseball bat, flashed two pairs of dagger-like incisors and snarled with all the venom he could muster. Now standing to his full height, with his coat of gold and brown cascading around him, he knew he looked as fierce as a bear.

With another roar, he saw the bravado on the faces of the dogs evaporate as they immediately backed away. They stared up at him with horror and as their arrogance diminished, so did their size. Not a tail or an ear stood alert upon their tiny forms and the fur on their backs seemed as flat as a cornfield after a cyclonic wind.

He demanded that they take him to their den at once and silently they conceded, glancing anxiously back at him as he followed them into the bushes.

Once in the den, the four dogs tried to keep a wide berth, but as the den was so tiny, this was difficult. They stumbled around him trying to find a space big enough to keep a decent distance between them and him. They were scared. He could smell it.

As he glared down at these tiny dogs, George felt his ego soar like a bird. Clearly, he was in charge now. They knew it. He knew it.

"Right, then," he growled, his confidence now reaching epic proportions, "Where the hell is your Alpha? I demand to see him at once!"

It was at that moment that the moon flung aside a fluttery cloud and shone down with full force upon an upturned wooden crate in the middle of the den. As the three male dogs slunk cautiously back into the bushes, the fourth dog, the female, jumped proudly up onto the crate. Glaring him straight in the eye she announced, "I, am the Alpha in charge!"

George was flabbergasted! He had expected a male dog: A big, male dog! Instead, the mini female fox terrier stood before him and seemed to have shed her fear within seconds of him invading their den. He couldn't believe it. He stepped back a pace to get a better view. "You?" he choked, "But you're just a little bitch?"

To his annoyance, she smiled. "Indeed, I am," she said raising herself to her full height, which although merely a quarter of a metre, was, he noted, much higher when you took into account her crate. "Clearly, you have spent too much time in the company of humans. In the dog world, females get to be in charge!"

As the moon reflected a beam of light into her huge brandy eyes, he felt cold shards of crystal shoot through him like shrapnel and cut right into the core of his newfound confidence.

His ears felt hot and itchy, but he resisted the urge to scratch them. Of course, he knew about equal rights. There were females in the army, both human and dog. However, his initial anger had been directed towards a dog called Charlie, so it was a male he had been expecting. Someone like Sid. But bigger. This turn of events completely floored him.

Yet again, he felt the fool and to his horror he found himself not only apologising for his mistake but actually trying to justify it. "Erm… yes… well, Charlie is a male's name surely? I heard the name mentioned in my garden and I assumed you were a male."

"I see," she replied, tossing her nose in the air, "and I presume that you are the highly esteemed war dog then? The one who I hear is too scared to come out of his house."

At once he remembered why he was here and the hair on his back rose to attention. He stepped back again to observe his enemy.

She stood tersely on short, stout legs; her hind legs splayed out behind a curvy rump. Although her body was splattered with black and white splodges, her long, thin jaw was the colour of golden butter. It protruded out from a ring of short black fur that shrouded her head and ended, mask-like, below her huge brawny eyes. She wore that head fur like a balaclava. Only her golden eyebrows and a streak of white that ran like a dart down the front of her jaw, broke up the effect.

Her black leather collar was studded with sharp, metal cones and if she'd been human, he would have expected a black leather jacket and a pair of dark sunglasses to top off the effect.

However, he noted with some amusement that her ears, though no doubt powerful, were extremely out of proportion to the rest of her size. They stood up high and proud, like huge, noble pyramids, but on a dog so small, they merely looked comical. Furthermore,

41

although she held her tail up to its fullest height to signal her confidence and aggression, he noted that the tip curled over her rump like a floppy feather duster. He was sure that this infuriated her. It was extremely feminine and distinctly out of sorts with the macho image she seemed to portray. Clearly, she could not control the tip of her tail and clearly, it was control that she thrived on.

He thought of Sadie who had a healthy balance of control and aggression, yet who had embraced her feminine side with pleasure. This foxy, he suspected, had no wish to reveal her vulnerability or her feminine side. He felt sure she regarded the latter as a weakness, despite her statement about equal rights in the dog world, and the human need for control.

To his horror, he found himself both intrigued and intimidated. It was an effect he disliked intensely, for how could such a tiny dog invoke such a complex array of emotions in him in one single minute of gracing him with her arrogant presence? He knew immediately that he was not dealing with the pampered pet he had envisaged. This foxy had seen some life and he knew she was a cunning and unpredictable enemy.

Despite his sudden anxiety, George managed to muster up some anger. He was not going to let this bitch intimidate him. He raised his ears and tail to signal his aggression and growled. He noted the hairs on Charlie's back flatten and although this signal of fear was barely visible, he felt some small measure of satisfaction.

Again, he recalled his mission. Glaring directly at Charlie he snarled, "Yes. I am the ex-army war dog you lot have been gossiping about. I've fought in wars for eight long years and seen horrors that you lot could never imagine!"

He sat back on his haunches and slammed his tail down on the ground causing a splattering of mud to flip onto his back. "How dare you send your little pack of pathetic miniatures onto my property to insult my intelligence with their ignorant remarks? If you had a bullet whizzing past your ears every two seconds you too would be scared! Damnit," he growled, as his anger escalated, "I've been a front-line fighter, detecting and inspecting bombs and weapons my whole life. I've seen my best friends mutilated with shrapnel, blown to pieces, and burnt to a cinder. My God, you lot haven't lived? You seem to have nothing better to do accept muck about in this poor excuse for a den and moan about your humans. Do you have any idea at all what being in the war means?"

He glanced down at the three little dogs on the floor and noted with pleasure their discomfort. None of them could look him in the eye and all of them seemed hell bent on licking or scratching some invisible irritation on their fur.

Charlie, however, remained upright, alert, and as still as a statue. Although her eyes had turned positively artic, her voice took on the tones of honey and he was reminded at once of the snakes in Ghan. "Well, Inspector – if that is what we call you for now – I apologise for the behaviour of my pack. However, their opinions were rather much based upon the abject fear they sniffed on your lawn."

She raised her eyebrows and he saw her smirk, but he allowed her to continue. She had at least raised his status by calling him Inspector, but if he wanted her to grovel, it seemed he was out of luck. Instead, she purred, "So if my pack are mistaken and you really are the brave war dog we have heard about, then please, do tell us exactly what it means to 'be in the war'."

George felt his heart skip a beat. Damn this foxy! She was not going to undermine his confidence after all he had been through. Now however, he felt stumped for words. How did he explain eight long years of war to this little lot? In fact, now he thought about it, why should he? "You and your ridiculous little pack would never understand," he snarled, "In fact I should save myself the bother and just rip the lot of you to pieces!"

Charlie remained unfazed by this comment and said, "Actually, Inspector, I think you may be right. I don't think we would understand."

For a second, she sounded quite genuine and although her eye mask still gave her the look of a hardened convict, he was surprised to see some small measure of respect in her eyes. His agitation subsided a bit, but it annoyed him that he took some pleasure in gaining her respect.

"So," she continued, "I guess that leaves you with two choices really. Either tear us apart or let us explain why we required the use of a war dog in the first place. I gather your skills were in detecting and inspecting and rumour has it that you were somewhat of a hero in your time."

He felt sure she stated the last part as if to imply he was old and past it, but he let this go. At least she was acknowledging his skills.

"I am afraid we are in rather a dilemma. Or at least one of my pack is." She glanced down at the young dog who wagged the tip of his tail gratefully. "It involves a murder of a human and a missing or murdered cat, and we are having great difficulty trying to resolve it. I am sure that your army skills would be of great use to us, and we would be honoured if you would help us." She paused and softened her gaze. "So perhaps you would like to decide on your next move, Inspector?"

By God, this Foxy is clever, he thought. On the one hand she was challenging him to a fight, whilst on the other, she was stroking his ego and playing on his natural sense of curiosity. She knew his pride had been affected by their comments, and she knew the safety of her pack depended on her ability to rectify all this without showing her fear. He slammed his tail down in frustrated fury and heard a small yelp from one of the dogs below.

He glanced down and saw he had smashed his tail onto the head of the young lad. The little dog stared up at him. As the moon shone down into his small chocolate eyes, he saw not hate or fear, but instead, hope. This was the lad who had sought his assistance, the young dog who had stood apart from the others and seemed to be of no importance to them, until their safety was at stake. As he stared angrily into the eyes of the dog, he saw the hope begin to wane, and so it was, in that instant, before all hope was lost, that George knew the choice he would make.

He relaxed his stance and lowered his ears to signal his decision and as he did so, a silence descended upon the pack. He sat there for a minute as the four dogs eyed him warily and it was then, just then, that the moon chose to cover her globe with a cloud.

Chapter 6

2200 hours

Standing on her crate, Charlie was nearly at eye level with George. He had only broken eye contact when he looked at the lad. Now a decision was made, she too sat down and told the others to do the same. He spoke at once, not wanting her to dominate the next course of events. It was up to him to show these dogs he was still boss, even if he was not going to attack them.

"Well, I admit I am intrigued." He paused for effect. "However, if I listen to your story and decide to detect and inspect, then I would like you all to know," again he paused, "that I do have an exceedingly good memory and I do not forget those who have shown me disrespect!" He glared down at the two male dogs who had offended him in his garden and then growled, "If any of you dare to cross me then I will have no hesitation in ripping out your throats!"

"Inspector," said Charlie, "I am sure my pack will bear that in mind. I am pleased you have decided to help us. So, if we are to crack on with the case, then I think we should first introduce ourselves. We do not know your name. Please, do tell us so we can ensure that we treat you with the utmost respect."

She lowered her jaw slightly and stared at him through hooded eyes. Despite her great speech, he still felt sure she was being sarcastic. Not only that, but he had never much liked introductions. The name George didn't seem war-like enough for him. Besides, there was no way he was letting these little psychos anywhere near his arse. If they expected a sniff they were out of luck. Visions of his crown jewels being ripped off and chewed up by a bunch of miniature mongrels flew through his mind. If he was going to die, it was not going to be via this method. His army comrades would be appalled!

He decided to evade the question and instead said, "I think for the purposes of this case, it would be appropriate if you all called me Inspector or Sir." He raised his ears to emphasise his point. All he heard was a quiet snigger from down below. Charlie swiftly intervened.

"Inspector, I'm sure we can accommodate your needs on that front," she spoke again in those honey tones, "But surely we ought to know your full name and of course how you came to inherit it. As you know, such information is polite in the dog world."

He cleared his throat and decided to answer quickly.

"My full name is George Penkins: Sergeant George Penkins. I am a K9 specialist in the detection of guns, bombs, and drugs. During my last post in Afghanistan, I was attached to the Royal Marine Corps." He raised his head higher. "My original human family descended from a long line of wealthy aristocrats, all with military backgrounds. They were breeders of German Shepherds, but since I was the only dog they felt suitable for the army, they named me after the Colonel. When I left for my first post in Iraq, I was escorted by Colonel George Penkins. Naturally, I am a thoroughbred!" He raised the hairs on his back to display an intricately woven mass of gold and black, and certainly he knew he portrayed a fine and noble stature.

Charlie nodded. "We are honoured to be in your company then, Inspector."

"Why didn't you go home to the autocrats after the war then?" said Sid, who seemed to have developed a rather large smirk on his face. George gritted his teeth.

"I did not return to the aristocrats, because after eight years I was a stranger to them. In fact, I was lucky to have even returned home. Most war dogs do not get that pleasure." He glared down at Sid.

"Sir," said the young lad, "that is so sad. All those poor dogs that died in the war, and for you to be not wanted anymore."

George noted that the lad seemed genuine in his response.

"Son, it's the way of the dog world. We do not choose our humans. They choose us. They also decide when we are to die. However, I am happy with my new human. She is kind, loving and considerate. Now tell me, young lad, what is your name and your story?"

The young dog stood up and wagged his tail proudly. He was taller than the other dogs, yet despite his height he seemed to project an aura of vulnerability that the others hid well. He wore a red leather collar, which was studded with fake diamonds, and although the collar suited him and contrasted well with his short black fur, it made him look a bit effeminate. Added to this, he had a graceful demeanour, which was aided by a long, sleek body and an earnest, handsome face. When he spoke, it was in high pitched, youthful tones that only emphasised his innocence.

"Sir, when I was born, I was the only black pup in the litter. When my human came to get me, he said he picked me out because I was as black as he was, with long legs to match." The little black dog pranced around in front of George as he proudly exhibited his legs.

George eyed the lad's legs and although long, they seemed to hang down like skinny, little twigs below his spindly, young body. He recalled the speed the lad had ran earlier and decided that looks were indeed deceiving.

"He told me I was a mini-fox terrier cross whippet and that I had Doberman in me because of my ginger paws and the ginger diamond on my bum." He turned at once and proudly raised his thin little tail. George had a full view of the diamond that sat splayed upon his scrawny rump.

"Indeed, the mark of a Doberman, Son. I see that now," said George, although he had difficulty hiding the doubt in his voice. He heard yet more sniggers from the other dogs and though he felt his irritation grow, he chose to ignore them. The lad seemed not to notice and continued his story.

"My human told me that his ancestors were African Zulu warriors and that I reminded him so much of them that he decided to call me Zulu." His tail wagged in pleasure and his eyes glistened with pride.

"Son," said George, "that is indeed an honourable name and certainly one to be proud of. I've heard of those Zulu warriors, and they were not a bunch to be messed with from what I gather."

George heard another snigger. He looked down and saw the Jack Russell. He was white, with ginger splodges and he had blubber of flab around his stomach. He noticed that each time the dog chuckled, the fat would jiggle about around him, a fact that did nothing but add to his horrid character. He recalled the comments that had been made about his weight when they were in his back garden. As the little Jack stood on his short, bandy legs and glared up at him with a pair of beady ginger eyes, George was reminded of a miniature piglet. However, he decided, it would be a gross insult to pigs to associate this dog with them.

"And what pray are you called?" he asked, his eyes darkening to reflect his contempt for this dog. The dog raised his ears and tail. His head barely reached the knees of George.

"I am a Jack Russel, Sir. My name is Rocky, and my humans are into martial arts."

George curled his lip and intentionally flashed a dagger-white tooth. But then he thought of something and burst out laughing. Swishing his bushy tail around in a frenzy, he purposefully slung a tail-full of dirt into the face of Rocky. "Oh my God," he bellowed, "please do not tell me that you are named after that fictional boxer in the movies? I mean, if that's so, then your humans certainly have a jolly good sense of humour don't they, eh?"

Rocky was clearly offended and raised his tail in anger. "How dare you joke at my expense," he growled, "I'll have you know that I am one of the best fighters in this neighbourhood and no matter how big or dangerous, I will do battle to the death with anyone! We Jacks never give up in a fight, Inspector."

George raised his eyebrows. "Oh really? Well, I guess that remains to be seen doesn't it, Rocky." At once he began fantasizing about ripping apart this fat little porker.

Before he could make any further comments, Sid stepped forward. His dirt-white fur curled tightly around his skinny body, yet his ears and facial hair hung down around his head in a shaggy mass. Any other dog like him might have been regarded as cute, but this one seemed dishevelled and un-kept.

He stunk of tobacco as well and he looked as if he'd not had his dinner for weeks. In fact, thought George darkly, he was sure he could sniff the faint smell of cannabis on the fur of that dog.

George recalled the fluffy pet mascots in Ghan who had a similar appearance, but unlike those dogs, Sid had nasty eyes. Through the mass of tangled hair on his face, they glared intensely at him.

"Inspector,' he growled, "my name is Sid, and I am a Cockerpoo."

"A what?" gasped George. "What in Dog's God is a Cockerpoo? Sounds extremely crude if you ask me."

Ignoring this remark, Sid stood up tall and proud. "A Cockerpoo is a cross between a Cocker Spaniel and a Poodle." He sat back down but despite this expression of pride, George noticed he evaded eye contact and instead scratched awkwardly at an ear.

George wagged his tail in amusement. "So basically Sid, you're a combination of those fancy, pom-pom dogs the humans parade around in shows. The ones they dress up in human clothes and who look like complete wimps; if you don't mind my saying."

Sid stood up and raised his tail in anger. "How dare you call me a wimp!" he growled. "I live with the hardest bunch of people in this neighbourhood. No one messes with them, and no one crosses me."

George rolled his eyes. "Not that horrid bunch of useless hooligans over the road I hope?" he snapped. He eyed the little dog more carefully. "A Cockerpoo, eh. Well, what will they come up with next, Sid? I wonder for what purpose you were bred. I was of the impression that breeds such as you were bred to be cuddly fur door mats for humans to play with or," he coughed, "take to the local beautician." He chuckled again. He was keen to find any way to put down this little snitch.

"Damn you," growled Sid, "I'm one of the most respected dogs in the neighbourhood. How dare you call me a doormat. I'm bred to fight, and I most certainly do not get cuddled, ever!" For a split-second Sid's eyes flitted to one side, and in that moment, he looked quite sad. George briefly wondered what kind of life he led. If Sid really did belong to the same gang of idiots who roared past his house, then he doubted the dog received much attention.

He obviously didn't receive much care. A good bath and a decent haircut might have at least helped with his appearance.

It explained his behaviour though. However, as he was such a horrid little character, George decided that there was no excuse for rudeness. This shaggy little hound had played a key role in mocking his army skills and George had no desire to try and understand it. As far as he was concerned, this mop of fur was still on his hit list, especially as he seemed so intent on putting down Zulu.

He turned his gaze towards Charlie who remained seated on her throne.

"And what of you, Miss Charlie?" he said, bowing his head in mock respect. "How did you come by your name?"

To his surprise Charlie turned her nose away and stared distantly at the ground. No one spoke. She seemed quite suddenly at a loss for words. She appeared to be contemplating her answer to this question, yet her shoulders sagged down as if she carried the weight of the world on them. However, before George could consider this, she suddenly sat back up to her full height and raised her ears.

"Inspector, have you ever heard of a drug called cocaine?"

"Of course, I have. Drugs were a part of my basic training. I can sniff any of them out, but my focus was on opium when I worked in Afghanistan."

Charlie looked impressed but he noted that her eyes darkened to reflect a mix of brandy and coke.

"Well, Inspector, I was initially bred by a drug baron. He specialised in the manufacture and sale of amphetamines. There were other drugs of course but cocaine was his favourite. He decided to call me Charlie, which is a nickname for cocaine of course, and naturally he took great pleasure in spiking my food with it."

She tossed her tail dismissively as if this was of no importance to her. "As for my breed, I am a mini-Fox Terrier cross, Border Terrier cross, Jack Russell cross Corgi." She paused for breath, which made sense, thought George. Stating her breed with all those crosses was a serious mouthful. "My siblings were sold, apart from my brother," she continued, "We were kept for the purpose of guard dog duties, ratting and general entertainment. That is until, Inspector, I decided to escape." She glared at him intensely as if challenging him for more questions.

However, George was at a loss for words. There was a haunted look in her eyes. Somehow, he knew that there was more to this story than she had revealed. He felt his heart contract. As he stared back at her, he felt a small smidgen of something familiar. A common bond perhaps, over something she felt unable to explain, for, like him, it was all too painful. He knew this foxy was tough, but behind that enamel exterior, she hid something soft and vulnerable. He would bet his left paw on it.

"After that," she continued, "I lived off the land and learnt to hunt animals. I survived for a while but in the human world pickings are slim. Many animals have moved on due to the decrease in land and water supplies. As a result, I was found one day lying in a ditch. I was cold, exhausted, and starving. I ended up in an animal shelter where I remained in a concrete cell for many months, until finally, I was adopted by a human."

As she paused for breath, George recalled the concrete cells the enemy were held in, and he wondered if the experience had sent her insane.

Before he could ponder this further, she barrelled her way back into his thoughts. "It's a rather boring existence, Inspector, so when I discovered this pack meeting up at night in these woods, I decided to join up with them. Now we meet each night, and as you say, just 'muck about', and moan about our humans." She raised her tail again to signify her offence at the remarks he had made when he initially arrived at their den.

George looked at the little pack as they stared up at him. He decided that they were more intriguing than he had originally thought. Certainly, they were more than the average fur pets that he had imagined. However, apart from Zulu, he realised that they were also cunning and vicious, and he decided that he would not trust them.

He glanced up at the moonlit sky. The trees stood high above him; their branches bare from the loss of autumn leaves. They seemed to erupt from the earth like the arms of a million dead soldiers, seeking a way to unearth themselves from their muddy grave.

As a gust of wind blew through the branches it was as if he could hear the shrieking wails of his beloved dead comrades. He felt a shiver sneak up his spine and wondered if he was about to make the biggest mistake in his life.

Chapter 7

2230 hours

The five dogs sat in silence for a minute. Each seemed to be contemplating something personal. George decided to break the silence.

"Well, I guess if I am to investigate this case then we ought to commence proceedings immediately." He sat up straight and raised his ears. "Exactly who has been murdered and why is this missing cat of such significance?" He directed this question at Zulu who then looked to Charlie for permission to speak. She nodded her head and he stood up at once. George noticed the tension in his tail and as the lad began his story, he stumbled over his words and spoke so quietly that his voice was barely audible.

"Sir, it's all been a huge mistake really. But I'm in big trouble now and so is my human." His eyes glanced around the den and into the night as if he was scared that some other unknown entity might hear him. "My human is in jail," he whispered, "We've both been accused of murder and I'm lucky to have escaped, but everyone thinks I'm guilty and that I did it. But, Sir, it wasn't my fault, and my human is innocent. He didn't kill the old bag next door, and no one knows if that stupid cat is dead or not. Now I'm in hiding and the neighbours are baying for my blood. We…"

George slapped his tail on the floor. The lad had turned into a quivering nervous wreck, and he could make no sense of this convoluted monologue.

"Son, I think you should slow down and tell me the story from the beginning. If I am to solve this case, then I need all the facts, every detail. Now sit down and start from the beginning and speak up, lad. I can hardly hear you."

Zulu sat but his worried expression remained. "Well, Sir, it all began about a week ago on the night of that great storm. You remember when the wind ripped through the village and tore down trees and stuff?"

"Yes, Zulu. I recall it well. There was much talk of it on the news. People were debating the effects of climate change." He decided to omit the part where he had hidden under the table all night in a quivering mass of fear. Every flash of lightning and clap of thunder had thrown him right back onto the battle ground.

Zulu continued, "Yes, exactly. Well, it started then. Actually, it started a bit before that, but it was then that things went very pear shaped for me and my human."

"Okay. So, what happened before the storm?"

"Well, Sir. My human is a policeman, and we live next door to a horrible lady and her vicious cat. At least, we did live next door to them. But anyway, that cat was my mortal enemy. She was always prancing about in the tree over-hanging my garden and showing off. She was always picking on me, Sir."

"That doesn't surprise me, Lad. Those cats can be nasty little beasts. I've had a few fights with them myself. But go on."

"She was a beautiful cat though. Very refined she was, but she knew it. She was always bragging about her being a pedigree, but she kept hissing at me and calling me a dirty, black mongrel. She was always insulting me, Sir, and we used to argue and hurl insults at each other all the time."

"Yes, I can fully understand your plight, Zulu. It's a common story. Cats and dogs are both predators and we like to remind each other who is boss. But what was the breed and name of this cat?

"She was an Egyptian Mau. She didn't look like other cats though. She looked more like a leopard. She had big pointy ears, dagger-like teeth and loads of black spots on a ginger coat. For a cat, she was quite big, really. Bigger even than Charlie. She said her name was Elizabeth and that she was named after the Queen."

"Mmm, the Queen, eh? Well, I am sure that the Queen would be extremely disappointed in such incorrigible, disgusting behaviour." George was a royalist. He had served many years fighting for this Queen.

"But, Sir, she used to swan about the place acting like the Queen all the time. She looked down on us dogs. I don't know if the human Queen would be disgusted because I heard that she parades around as if she owns us all too."

George shifted on his rump. He felt uncomfortable discussing the Queen in this manner. The army had told him that she was the symbol of England and he had fought a war for her and the country. Still, he had been disappointed in the outcome of the war and had begun to doubt the point in it all. He had never seen the Queen come to Afghanistan for example and though her sons and grandsons flew in on occasion they were usually heavily protected, unlike his comrades in the lower echelons of the army. He decided to reserve his judgement and ignore Zulu's comments about the value of the Queen.

"Inspector, I hated her so much in the end. I used to bark and bark until my human told me off. But he didn't know that smarmy, arrogant cat was teasing me. She told me that all dogs were worthless bags of poo and that I should have been killed at birth. She was always saying that she could kill me but every time I went near her, she would leap back onto her tree and over the fence into her garden. I tell you, I really did want to kill her, but it wasn't me that did it, Sir. I promise you that."

"Did what, Zulu?" George felt his interest lift.

"Well, kill her, Sir. After that storm, the wind blew down a few of the fence posts that separated our two gardens. It left a gap big enough for me to squeeze through and get her. Elizabeth's human was always coming around to complain to my human about my barking. That old woman was a wrinkly old hag. She didn't even care that my human is a policeman. But even so, he was still worried about me barking, so he would tell me off. He said if I didn't stop barking then the Council might make him put me down. He would get so upset about it because he didn't want to lose me."

Suddenly, everyone grew tense. Clearly, they didn't like the words 'put down'. George understood how they felt. He knew that dogs in the army who had served their time would often just disappear. Rumour had it that they were 'put down'. Apparently, it was cheaper to do that, and George recalled feeling damn angry about it. In fact, when he knew he was losing the plot on his last post, that had been one of his fears. He had been lucky, but many of his war dog friends had not been so fortunate. He slammed his tail down on the floor in anger.

"So, this old wrinkly bat next door wanted rid of you then and this was before any murder had occurred?"

Zulu sighed and nodded his head. "It just wasn't fair, Sir. That horrible cat should have been the one put down. Then after the storm, the old hag next door kept coming around and demanding my human fix the fence. She said her beloved Elizabeth was in danger because I could slip through the fence and kill her. But Sir, I wouldn't do that. I mean, I wanted to kill her. We all did." He glanced warily at the others. "I told these guys what I was going through, and even they said they wanted her dead. In fact," he paused, "they even said that they would help me do it." He looked at the other dogs for confirmation. However, for some reason every one of those miniatures looked away or down at the ground. It seemed, he noted, that they had no wish to confirm their part in any plans to kill the cat.

An uncomfortable knot grew inside George's stomach. He glared at the other three dogs. "Well," he demanded, "is this true? Were you all in on some plan to kill this cat or not?"

Naturally, Charlie spoke first. Where previously she had been lying flat on her crate listening to Zulu, she now stood up and raised her tail until it curved full circle over her back. With a piercing glare, she said, "Well of course we wanted to kill her. I mean who wouldn't? She thought she was a cut above the rest of us that cat. She kept prancing around in her tree claiming she was connected to some Egyptian Queen whilst calling us filthy inbred mutts with two heads and no brains. Zulu's right. She was nasty and vindictive but too gutless to take us on!"

George raised his ears. "Ah. So, you lot had met this feline too then?"

"Of course," she continued in full swing, "When Zulu told us of his plight we marched right on up to her back fence and demanded she come down and face us. But she just sat in that tree and taunted us all. Of course, we wanted her dead. None of the dogs around here liked her. You just ask them. Some couldn't get out of their gardens or just wouldn't, but she sure as hell made sure she snuck over to theirs and peed her feline stink in their gardens."

She sniffed her nose in disgust and continued, "After the storm, about three days to be exact, Elizabeth disappeared, and it was then that the old bag went around to our lad's house and accused both him and his human of murder. She was adamant that they had both killed Elizabeth that night and she reported it to the Council and the police. She even got the neighbours involved and both Zulu and his human began receiving death threats. Zulu even alleges that there was a lump of human poo pushed through their letterbox. Of course, the police couldn't do anything. I mean, how could they?" She arched her eyebrows and stared through her balaclava. "There was no body, so there was no murder, was there?"

She sat back down as if she was satisfied with her explanation.

George, however, was not. Now it seemed that there was a list of suspects as long as his front paws, including this motley pack of dwarfs he sat with. Clearly, there was more to this story. Why for example was Zulu the accused? Yes, he hated the cat, but apart from the barking, what evidence did this neighbour have against him. He would have to tread cautiously here. The lad did not look like a murderer but there was clearly something amiss. He needed more facts.

"Right, then," he said, standing up and beginning to pace thoughtfully around Charlie's crate. "From what I can gather so far, with regards to the cat, Zulu here is our primary suspect. He lived next door to her. We know they were arch enemies and the neighbour accused him of her murder. The very fact that he hates this missing cat means he has motive."

Zulu looked glum and swished his tail around listlessly.

"Furthermore," said George, "he had opportunity. There was a gap in the fence. However, without a body there is no murder as such."

Zulu sat down as relief washed over his face.

"So," continued George, as he turned suddenly towards the lad, "Exactly where were you on the night in question?"

Zulu stood up at once, stiff and alert, as if he were about to salute an officer. "Inspector, I was asleep. Tucked up in bed all cosy, I was." He wagged his tail as if pleased with his explanation and immediately sat down.

George noticed how quickly the lad spoke. He was too abrupt, had sat back down too quickly and there was something in his demeanour that suggested he was hiding something. "I see," he replied with a doubtful tone, "So, if you were tucked up in bed, all cosy as you say, exactly who were you with and can they verify your location?"

Zulu flattened his ears and stared down at the ground. "Well, Sir, it's difficult, isn't it? I mean, I was asleep with my human, but, as he was asleep too, how can he confirm if I was asleep?"

"Well, lad, that is the twenty-four-thousand-dollar question, isn't it? How do we know if whilst your human was asleep you did not sneak outside, kill the cat and then return to your bed as usual?"

George didn't like confronting the little dog like this, but he knew he had to and for some reason, he was beginning to enjoy himself. He felt like he had grown back his shiny, young army nose, but this time, instead of creeping cautiously down 'IUD valley' (roads with suspected improvised unexploded devices), he was pacing around like a judge in a courtroom TV drama. Yet again, like in the valley, all eyes were on him, the army hoping he'd find the bomb, the enemy hoping he wouldn't. One thing he knew for sure, with his army nose back in action, he was not about to make any mistakes. Someone's life was at stake here and the enemy or culprit was still at large, possibly pointing a gun at him, albeit only metaphorically, but the feeling was just the same.

This investigative role was all too familiar and that was why he knew, without any doubt, that for some reason, Zulu was lying.

This was confirmed when the young dog stood up and began to pace anxiously around Charlie's crate. His thin black tail curled tightly around his rump and the whites of his eyes flashed guiltily at George before glancing fearfully at the other three dogs.

"But, Sir," he stammered, "I really was in bed. I didn't even go outside when I heard Elizabeth yowling."

George's ears perked up and his tail grew tense. "You mean you actually heard the cat yowling? Well, why didn't you say so before? If you heard the cat yowling then maybe others heard too, in which case we have an approximate time of death... or rather time of missing cat! This puts a whole new perspective on the case. What time did you hear this, lad, and speak up I can hardly hear you again?"

"Inspector," Zulu now yelled, as if responding to the demands of a Sergeant in the army, "it was just about the time when the moon had made her way about three quarters of the way across the sky." He sat back down, too quickly and again, with a strange, evasive look in his eye.

George shifted on his rump. The lad was turning into a nervous wreck, yet for some reason, he did not think it was because he had committed a crime. He wanted to be gentle on Zulu, but his training had taught him to leave no stone unturned. He had been trained to inspect everyone, even if they looked innocent. His time in the army had taught him that even young lads could be hiding ticking time bombs under their cloaks. He also knew that those same lads had been protecting their elders.

He decided to continue with the direct approach, even if he did sound a bit like a bully. Persistence on his part had always increased a suspect's fear, and although he hated doing this to the young dog, he knew that fear would expose the truth in the end.

"Well, now..." he pondered, "By my calculations that would be about 3am in the morning. So, lad," he suddenly demanded, "exactly what did you hear and why did you not go out and investigate?"

Zulu scratched his ear and looked away. Clearly, he felt like some sort of wimp for staying in bed. "Inspector," he pleaded, "I was so snuggly and warm, and I'd already had a terrible night."

He glanced furtively at the others again and George noticed that they all had the look of guilt about them. "Why should I go out investigating when she was always yowling and mewing at night?" he continued, his tone now becoming high-pitched and defensive, "I mean sometimes I went out and told her to shut it, but that night I didn't. Besides, I didn't want to get put down, so I stayed in bed!"

"I see." George rolled his eyes. "So, had you done your duty as guard dog, lad, then you may well have been witness to the very murder that you have been accused of. What's more, we are still no clearer on whether either you or your human actually committed this crime, because you have yet to provide me with a witness to your whereabouts. Maybe you dropped off to sleep and your human killed the cat, Zulu."

At this point, Charlie growled. She stood back up on her box and raised her tail impatiently. "Enough! Enough of this nonsense, Inspector! Zulu here is not our suspect and you are just wasting our time interrogating him like this."

Zulu stopped pacing and breathed out a loud sigh of relief. He looked at Charlie and wagged the tip of his tail gratefully.

The whiskers on George's nose bristled. He had been proud of his detecting skills and felt that yet again this smug little bitch was trying to undermine him.

"Miss Charlie," he growled, "If I am to inspect and detect then I ask the questions. I am the expert here, remember?" he raised himself to his full height in a bid to reassert his authority.

"Nevertheless," retorted Charlie, who was clearly not intimidated, "Your questions are irrelevant. It is simply impossible for Zulu to commit a murder, never mind attack that stupid cat."

George sighed and sunk down on his haunches resignedly. "I see, Miss Charlie. Well do tell me how you, if you were not with Zulu at the time, can be so sure of this?"

Charlie flicked her tail and sniffed. "Well, it's obvious, isn't it? Just look at him."

All eyes turned towards Zulu and Sid gave a quiet snigger. The young dog sat down, and his shoulders slumped over his quivering hind legs. He pawed at the muddy ground absently and stared at it.

"Well," questioned Charlie, "is there anything about our lad here that makes you question his ability to kill, Inspector?"

George stared intensely at Zulu, but this was more for effect, to get back at Charlie, than to prove that the lad was no killer. He was certainly hiding something and that something could be the killer. But now the lad looked so defeated and rejected, he felt sorry for him. He remembered his war training experiences though and decided to stick to his guns and ensure this foxy did not get the upper paw.

"Well, he does have a look of innocence about him, I'll admit. But mark my words," he growled, "I have stared innocence in the face many times, only to be sadly disappointed." He glared at Charlie and growled, "Psychopaths, often have many charms and disguises, Miss Charlie, and that, is exactly why they get away with murder." He slammed his tail down on the muddy ground and raised his ears triumphantly.

To his horror, Charlie burst out laughing. In fact, she was so amused that she fell onto her stomach and bellowed into her paws. Sid and Rocky followed suit until there was nothing but sniggering and tail wagging all round – except for Zulu, who gave a quiet little growl followed by a hiccup and a sob.

"What, may I say, is so damn amusing?" demanded George.

Charlie was now laughing so hard that she had difficulty getting out her words. However, she quickly regained her composure and yelled at George as if he were a total idiot. "Inspector, look! Just look! Zulu is a runt – the runt of the litter, for God's sake. He couldn't kill a fly let alone kill a great, vicious cat!"

Immediately Zulu stood up. His lanky stick legs were a stiff as arrows and the fur on his back glistened with anger. "How dare you all laugh at me!" he yelled, "I am not a runt, and I can too, kill a fly!"

Rocky managed to stop laughing and replied, "Oh come now, Zulu. You know damn well you can't kill a fly. I mean, I've seen you lad." He fell back onto his rump, his tiny teeth gleaming through his ginger jaws as he continued to chuckle.

"Seen me?" Zulu said, his voice all high pitched and defensive, "What do you mean?"

"Well, I've seen you snap at flies, and believe me, I know you could kill them, but you don't. You purposely avoid grabbing them in your jaws. You miss them by an inch, and everyone knows it." He wagged his tail in a frenzy, clearly pleased with this new assault on Zulu's ego.

"That's a lie, Rocky, and you know it!" Zulu pawed at the ground furiously. "I have killed flies… I have so."

George realised he had been gritting his teeth. His jaw throbbed with pain. "Oh, for God's sake you lot, shut up. I get the picture okay!" Now he felt sorry for the lad. Being the runt of the litter was no picnic. It was a cause for huge embarrassment, for no dog liked to admit that he lacked the initial will to survive and that necessary killer instinct. Zulu was still sobbing and whittling on about flies.

"Calm down, lad," he commanded, "Swallowing flies is not exactly my cup of tea either. They're disgusting dirty little insects who wallow in excrement all day, and anyone who idles their time away eating them no doubt suffers from severe bouts of verbal diarrhoea." He hurled a vicious glance at Rocky and continued, "Furthermore, there is nothing wrong with runts. In fact, I have served in the army beside many a runt," he lied, "and I can tell you now that they are the most loyal and honest dogs I have ever had the pleasure to be in the army with. Although I'll admit," he paused, "they're not usually in the killer sector, but they do have other skills. Skills which make them worthy of any military dog."

He gave Charlie a filthy look. Evidently, she had been the Alpha pup and he had no doubt that she had been the first to latch her jaws onto her mother's teat and the last to let go. Such was the nature of the selfish number one. Still, she seemed to want the last word.

"Well, now that it's glaringly obvious to you, Inspector, what do you suggest? I mean, clearly none of us are suspects or we wouldn't have asked you to solve this case, would we?" She raised her eyebrows and her artic eyes glared through her mask.

However, George still felt suspicious. He knew that Zulu was hiding something, and he also recalled how neither Rocky nor Sid had wanted him on the case.

In fact, all three of those dogs had been idling their time around the den when he had initially arrived. They were certainly in no rush to help Zulu.

Yet Charlie, who seemed like the biggest psychopath he had ever met, had defended the lad, albeit by further assaulting his ego. But still, she had put a halt on the interrogation. *Why,* he thought. Did she fear that Zulu might spill the beans and reveal the true culprit if he had continued to question the lad? He let out a huge sigh and stared up at the moon. He scratched his ear thoughtfully and then turned to Zulu.

"Lad, I don't think you did kill Elizabeth. But something still bothers me. The old bag next door seemed adamant that you killed her. In fact, she even accused your human of it. If there was no body, then why was she so convinced of your guilt?"

As the moon shone softly down into the chocolate eyes of Zulu, George saw a flicker of fear. The lad glanced anxiously at the other dogs who had become strangely silent and who were all glaring at Zulu. As he pawed at the floor, he stammered out a reply, but he spoke so softly, that George barely heard him. "Sir, it was the blood you see. When the neighbour came round to ask the whereabouts of her cat, both me and my human were standing at the door, and we were both covered in blood."

Chapter 8

2300 hours

George rolled his eyes and dropped down to the floor in despair. He rubbed his forehead wearily and tried to muster up some energy to listen to yet more of this story. He was feeling quite exhausted. After six months of lazing about eating and sleeping, he felt his mental faculties had diminished. Besides, the war had been a straight-forward affair. There was one enemy – anyone with a black beard basically – so there had been no need to analyse the motives of everyone involved.

Still, he was curious. These dogs were shifty looking characters, and they were clearly hiding something. Certainly, this Charlie was no fool. Maybe she had a secret plan to set him up – blame the war-crazed dog for killing the cat and her horrible human. For some while he lay on the floor pondering all this. Clearly, he would have to keep his wits about him although the temptation to walk off now tugged at his tail. He decided to stay though, for the sake of the lad. He felt sure that Zulu was innocent.

Blood or no blood there was more to this story than the obvious. He sat up and raised his ears, his nose ever alert for any suspicious smells from the others.

He sighed. "So, the old bat next door came around and saw you and your human covered in blood. Exactly why were you both standing at the door with blood on you, Zulu?"

Zulu sat back, flattened his ears, and curled his tail around his body. His legs started to quiver, and his eyes darted around nervously. He glanced up at Charlie with a hopeful look in his eyes, but she looked away. Rocky sniggered as did Sid.

"Well go on then, Zulu," chimed Rocky, "Tell the Inspector all about it."

Zulu remained hunched over his paws and now stared intensely at the muddy floor.

"Well come on, lad," demanded George, "Look alive now. You claim your innocent so why so pensive?"

Zulu glanced quickly up at George. His small chocolate eyes seemed to shimmer with tears and George noticed he had a look of both horror and shame about him. Sid and Rocky wagged their tails in amusement.

"Sir, "he whispered, "It was all a big mistake really. Sort of an accident, but not, if you get my drift."

"No, Zulu, I don't get your drift. You say you and your human were covered in blood. Why?"

Zulu glanced at the others and George sensed that he was hoping they would stand by him on this. When he spoke, it was with a nervous tremor. "Erm… well that night… the night Elizabeth went missing… well… I hadn't been in bed all night, Sir. I had snuck out again to see the others as usual." George felt a stab of self-satisfied smugness. So, he had been right. The lad had been hiding something. "My human was asleep," continued Zulu, "and that night, well, that night was supposed to be my big night." At this Rocky and Sid began to laugh, and George felt his irritation with them grow. The poor lad seemed to be a constant butt of their jokes.

"Go on lad," he said gently as he glared viciously at the others.

Zulu pawed at the floor and continued, "Sir, I had been with the pack for three months by then. But to belong to a pack you have to learn how to hunt and stuff. If you can hunt, then you can be a fully-fledged member of the pack."

George looked perplexed. "But lad, you've all got homes and shelter. You've got humans who feed you. What need have you to hunt?"

Zulu looked cautiously at Charlie who was sitting up alert on her crate and glaring at him.

"Sir, I really wanted to belong to a pack. It's every dog's dream isn't it – to be able to hunt and live off the land? I mean, I love my human, but what if something happens to him and I end up homeless? I wouldn't know how to survive. Now with all this murder stuff I actually am homeless, and I've got no one to feed me so hunting is obviously a useful skill, isn't it?" he looked at Charlie pleadingly, "Isn't that true, Charlie. You said it was vital we all learnt to hunt?"

Charlie gave a flick of her tail and glared at George. "Yes, Zulu. When I lived off the land I would have died if I had not known how to hunt. Luckily, I already had some ratting experience, otherwise I would have died. That, Inspector, is why I insist on my pack learning the basics." She raised her ears and gave George a filthy look.

Yet again, he felt his heart plummet to the ground. Still, he could not argue with her logic. If the lad was now homeless then he was clearly in need of some basic hunting skills.

"Okay, lad. So, you had to learn how to hunt, and that night was your 'big night'." He glared at Charlie. "Go on, lad."

"Okay, "continued Zulu, "Well after three months I was at level two in my training. I passed level one and level two with flying colours."

"And what does level one and level two involve?" George asked. He was curious now.

"Well, Sir," continued Zulu, who seemed to have become visibly more relaxed, "At Level one, Charlie says that you have to learn to be like the prey. To understand your prey, you have to pretend to be them and after that, you know them so well that you can hunt them down instantly. Actually, I was really good at level one, wasn't I, Charlie?" he said wagging his tail proudly. "I could out-run all the pack and they had a testing time trying to catch me. But Charlie said I had to get caught so I could understand what it felt like to be attacked."

George felt his irritation grow. He knew this had not been a part of his training when he learnt how to hunt the enemy. It seemed highly unnecessary and sounded suspiciously like bully tactics.

"Go on, Son," he said.

"So anyway, sometimes I let them all catch and attack me and…" but before he could finish, Charlie cut in and snapped, "Zulu! Remember I can catch anyone. There was no letting me catch you. I caught you fair and square and no arguments!" She glared at the little black dog, and he hunkered back down on his haunches. George noticed his back legs start to tremble again, but he continued with his story.

"Oh, err, yeah. I did lose a lot of the time," he conceded, "but then I had to learn how to fight off Charlie and the others. And when I learnt that, well then I moved onto level two training."

Charlie rolled her eyes. "Yes, well you were very good at level one, Zulu. You were certainly a challenge what with those long legs of yours and you did very well…" she paused and glared through her balaclava, "at playing the victim."

George felt like he had been stabbed with a knife. By Gods, he thought, was there no end to this bitch's nasty arrogant tirade? Clearly the lad was proud of his achievements, yet she and the others seemed to want to put him down constantly. He felt a need to stick up for the lad.

"Zulu, it sounds like you did exceptionally well in your training. Defensive manoeuvres are highly valued in the army. If you passed level one and with dogs as your enemy then I think you deserve a medal." He threw a hateful glare at the others. "Now go on, Son. You say you passed level one and two. What is level two?"

Zulu looked pleased. He looked up at George as if he was his new-found hero. George felt his heart break a little. The young dog continued, "Level two is stalking, Sir, sniffing out and sneaking up on the prey. Getting right up close to them so they don't know you're there. So, you can jump them and then eat them all up. That's where I got to. I passed level two and moved onto level three. I could sniff and stalk mice, rats, moles and birds and I was really good, wasn't I Charlie?" He wagged his tail proudly and Charlie seemed to accept this without comment.

To George, she clearly preferred level one, where she evidently enjoyed chasing and attacking the lad. Her need for domination and control was pathological and George wondered why Zulu had remained with these horrible dogs for so long. Despite this thought, he still had more questions.

"So, Zulu, on the night the cat went missing, you say it was your big night. What do you mean?"

"Yes, Sir. I was about to commence level three training."

"And this was the same night that resulted in you and your human being woken up in the morning covered in blood. The very same night that Elizabeth disappeared?"

"Yes," said Zulu, "When the old bag saw us that morning, she accused us of murder and said my human must have buried Elizabeth somewhere."

"Well, Zulu, I must admit, if I stood at the door and saw such a bloody sight then I too would have concluded the same. Clearly, she thought you had been busy all night burying the body and had not thought to clean yourselves up before answering the door."

"But it was so not like that, Sir. I mean we didn't even realise we had blood on us. Well... I suppose I did, but I kind of forgot because I was so stressed out when I went to bed. And then that stupid old hag knocked us up at dawn. We were both half asleep and we didn't think to look at ourselves."

"Okay, Son. So, what was with the blood then?"

The three dogs chortled, and Zulu once again looked down in shame. But still he continued, "Well it was cold that night, Sir bitterly cold. My human knew I felt the cold because I'm thin and don't have much hair. So, in preparation he bought me a new fleecy jumper. That night, before he went to bed, he insisted I wear it. But it was a bright white fleece and although I wanted to wear it, I knew it wouldn't be good for hunting in the dark, and I knew that I probably looked like a right ponce in it. I protested and tried to wriggle out of it, but it just made my human more determined. In the end, I had to give up and go out to meet the pack wearing my new white fleece."

At this, the other three dogs fell about in near hysterics, and it took all of George's strength not to rip them apart with his jaws. He gave a low menacing growl instead, which did enough to stop them in their tracks and regain their composure. They sat up alert and ready for the next part of the story. Zulu, of course, was still looking ashamed, but he plucked up the courage to continue.

"So, anyway," he now whispered, "I approached the pack in my new white fleece and of course it being my big night at level three and all, well they just all fell about laughing. They said I looked like a right little wimp. But then they said that we would go on with the test anyway. That maybe rats and mice couldn't see white, and as I was good at stalking, then maybe I would be able to do the job."

"The job?" said George, as he raised his eyebrows.

"The kill, Sir. That night was the night that I had to make my first kill."

"Okay, Son. Go on." George felt his interest lift.

"So, off we went in search of some prey. And, anyway, we, I mean I, found a rat."

"Yes, yes, go on." George felt his heart speed up a bit.

"So, I crept down really low, Sir, and watched the rat carefully as Charlie had taught me and I was all ready to do the jump. I really was. I mean, I really, really was."

George felt his excitement grow. His hunter instinct was beginning to emerge as he recalled the thrill of the hunt in the army. He couldn't help but want to hear the gory details and he felt impatient with the lad's reluctance to get to the point.

"Well go on, Son." He noticed yet more sniggers from the pack below.

"But then I started to think about that rat and how she probably had a little family who were waiting for her at home. I knew I wasn't supposed to think like that, but I did. I had already eaten a big dinner that night, so it seemed such a waste." His eyes looked up at George as if pleading for his support. "Then I felt sad for her, and I just froze. I couldn't move. I couldn't kill her, Sir, and I couldn't get through to level three!"

77

As the moon gleamed down upon the face of Zulu, he looked like a rabbit caught in the glare of a pair of car headlights. The shame leached through him. George realised that the lad was indeed a true runt and evidently no murderer. But still, why was he covered in blood? It was this question that he posed to Zulu who yet again glanced at the others in fear.

"Well, the next thing I knew, Charlie jumped the rat and ripped out her throat and suddenly Sid and Rocky were upon her as well. They were all clawing and biting her... that poor rat. They were like vultures, Sir. They tore her to pieces until she was a bloody pulp. By the time they had finished, she was dead. I wished then I had tried to save her. I didn't want her dead. But I couldn't move. Like a complete coward, I just stood there and watched." At this Zulu collapsed on the floor and began to sob. Clearly the memory of it all and the guilt was too traumatic for the lad.

George was horrified. He had never known a dog to be so sensitive. He had trained in the army, and he knew that not all dogs were cut out for it, but this story and this dog seemed to cut him to the core. The other dogs? Well dogs were dogs he supposed. He couldn't blame them for their hunter instinct, but to him, Zulu was a complete mystery.

"Well, what happened next then, Lad," he asked.

Zulu stopped sobbing and although he sat back up, he seemed reluctant to go on. He wrapped his tail around his rump and stared glumly at the floor. At one point, he flung a hateful glare at Rocky, who swished his tail casually and looked away. George glanced at Charlie and even she looked guilty, her ever arrogant tail now slumped down on her crate like a hairy snake. Something here was going on and George was damned if he was going to leave the lad alone with it all.

"Well, obviously there's an ending to this story. Any of you have the guts to tell me more?" he demanded.

Charlie flicked her tail in a sort of pseudo casual manner. She raised her nose haughtily and said, "Well I think Rocky should be the one to tell you the next part. Don't you think so, Rocky?" She arched her eyebrows and glared at him with her brandy eyes.

Rocky gave a nervous little laugh and looked up at George warily. Then suddenly he must have decided that he was well within his rights to be amused and he stood up at once to his full quarter of a metre tall.

"Well, for God's sake," he growled, "The lad had been in training for long enough. He wanted to be a part of our pack, but he froze. He needed to toughen up and grow some balls. I just teased him a bit."

"Hmm? How so?" quizzed George raising his ears. "Exactly how did you tease him, Rocky?"

Rocky cleared his throat. "Well, he was just standing there, frozen like a little snowman in his pure white fleece. We just… erm… well, I just thought it would be a laugh to give him the sacrilegious medal anyway. The blood-of-the kill." He paused and looked shiftily at Sid. "In short, Inspector, I threw the dead rat at him, and it landed on his new white fleece and then I went over and rubbed the rat blood all over his coat. There! I've said it. I covered our lad in the blood of the rat. That was the last we saw of him that night, for it was then that he raced off home with his tail between his legs. Sir, we don't tolerate weakness in the dog world and Zulu was acting weak. He needed to be taught a lesson!"

As Rocky slammed his tail upon the muddy floor, George gave out such a vicious growl that the trees above him seemed to tremble. He lunged towards Rocky and flung him onto his back. He was just about to rip out Rocky's throat when in the distance he heard Zulu yell, "Stop! Just stop, Inspector!"

Out of the corner of his eye he saw Zulu's pleading face. It was only because of that, because he valued the lad so much, that he relinquished his grip on Rocky's throat. But damnit, he thought, he was losing patience with these horrible dogs.

In a short time, he had grown fond of the lad, but he knew not how he was ever going to like these other dogs. For the sake of Zulu, he withdrew. But he slammed his tail down like a sledgehammer onto Rocky's stomach, just to ensure that the dog knew he meant business.

Chapter 9

2330 hours

George took a deep breath to stop him-self from tearing apart the whole pack. He couldn't believe how they had acted towards Zulu. Not only did they bully him relentlessly but due to their actions, he was now implicated in a murder he had clearly not committed. Furthermore, if Zulu had run home to his human and the cat had gone missing at 3am, then these other dogs were still suspects. He knew the physical rush of euphoria that followed a kill. Maybe these dogs had decided to continue in their killing frenzy and murder the cat. Either that or scare the cat into disappearing.

However, he had yet to hear about the murder of the old woman. He had become so engrossed in the details of the cat that he had ignored the second murder. He realised that there was more to this story. He doubted that these dogs had murdered a human. If they had, they would have needed an incredibly good reason. Charlie though, seemed to have a million reasons. She hated humans, but to kill one might be a stretch.

He decided he would need more facts. But before he asked Zulu to continue his story, he made sure that the others were all aware that if any further attacks on the young dog's confidence and skills occurred, then the lad would not stop him from tearing them to pieces. He told them that he was disgusted with their behaviour and that they would now have to ensure that they too could prove their innocence in the case of the missing cat. If he then discovered that they had anything to do with its death, then he would kill them and bury their bodies beneath Charlie's crate.

It took him five minutes to calm down and regain his wits. Rocky, meanwhile still lay on the muddy floor curled up in a ball, whilst he nursed his throbbing stomach. George felt nothing for the dog. He noted that none of the other dogs except Zulu were prepared to stick up for Rocky. Sid and Charlie remained seated, but they avoided eye-contact with George. Their ears lay flat on their foreheads and George sniffed the fear emitting from their fur. He felt satisfied that he had at least scared them, but he wondered if they would ever change. He decided that whatever the outcome of this case, he would ensure that he kept a close nose on their behaviour.

He turned to Zulu who was also seated. His ears remained upright and alert though and for once he seemed to show no fear. The lad stared up at him and his eyes shone with renewed hope. George told him that there was no shame in being unable to make his first kill. "It is not unusual, Zulu. Killing other animals for fun or for a test is not normal procedure. For a start, you have to be hungry, extremely hungry. Then you have to accustom yourself to observing your relatives kill and then get used to eating that type of food. None of those factors were applicable to you. No doubt, if you had continued with your training though, and perhaps gone a few days without your dinner, you may well have found that killing for food is easy.

"Unlike humans, most of us don't kill for fun, Zulu or to fill some underlying, pathological need for power," he glared at Charlie. "We tend to take what we need until we are hungry again. That is the law in the animal kingdom."

He noted the discomfort that now emitted from the fur of the other dogs. Apart from Zulu, they all looked guilty, and their tails hung down behind them like limp, little ropes. Having made his point, he decided that he should gather more facts.

"So, Zulu, if we are to solve this case quickly, then I need to know more. Tell me what happened when you left the pack that night."

Zulu sat and told the Inspector how he had raced through the park like a rocket, crashed through the dog-flap and arrived at his home panting and dying of shame. He felt so distraught that he forgot about the blood on his fleece. All he wanted to do was curl up in bed and snuggle up against the big chocolate feet of his beloved human. He fell into a fitful sleep and although he heard Elizabeth yowling, her screams were embedded in garish scenes of blood and the splattering of rat flesh, which oozed into his eyes and slid down his nose. As he wriggled up the bed to curl up against the chest of his human, he was awoken by a sound resembling the chopping of an axe against wood. As both he and his human came to, they realised it was someone banging loudly on the front door. So loud in fact, that it woke up half the street.

"It was the old bat next door, Sir, and she was furious when she saw us. My human had blood all down the front of his white pyjama top, and he hadn't brushed his hair or had a shower, so he looked a right mess. He was still half asleep when he answered the door, so he never looked at himself or me.

Then she saw me in my bloody white fleece, and she started screaming at us. She was like a wild cat herself standing there in her stinky old dressing gown, her slippers, with her straggly, grey hair streaming behind her. She said Elizabeth hadn't come for her bowl of cream that morning and she had found her collar in the back-garden. She called us murdering mongrels and said that she always knew my human was capable of murder." Zulu got up and started to pace around the den franticly as he relayed yet more of his story.

"Then she said the whole neighbourhood hated him because he was black and had a black beard. She screamed at him, Sir, and hurled insults I could never repeat. She told him that everyone thought he was a terrorist because he had a black beard and that he had black people visiting him in the dead of the night. She was so loud that all the neighbours came out of their houses to watch. Then she turned to them and started screaming at them to come and look at us, and that we were both covered in blood and that we had murdered her beautiful Elizabeth."

By then, Zulu had widened his pace and was trotting angrily around Charlie's crate. He spoke in rapid, breathless tones. He was making George feel dizzy and nauseous. He told the lad to sit down, and Zulu conceded with obvious reluctance. He had clearly not finished his story though.

"Sir, the neighbours looked at us really suspiciously then. One old man came over and saw all the blood. He yelled out to the neighbours that it was true and that the old bat must be right about us being murdering mongrels. He told my human that he was disgusted and that he should go back to his own country where murderers like him belonged.

"It was terrible. My poor human couldn't get a word in, and he just stood there in shock. He had no way to explain the blood on him or on me. The old hag then stormed off saying she was calling the newspapers and the police and that she was going to make sure that I got put down and my human went to jail for animal cruelty.

84

"When my human finally got the nerve to slam his door shut, all the neighbours were still staring and nodding their heads in disgust. Some of them started yelling, 'Shame, shame on you', and another shouted, 'Animal abuser. We don't tolerate animal abuse in this country!'"

George listened to the story with growing horror. But his horror was not directed at the neighbours and the old bat. Instead, he felt a familiar stab of anger in his heart. Zulu had said that his human had a black beard and was a suspected terrorist. George hadn't realised that before. He decided to ask, just to be sure. If this was the case, then George had no doubt that his human had been the one to murder the cat. The Taliban had black beards and they had killed many of his friends both human and dog. He would not put anything past a black-bearded man or a suspected terrorist, especially the murder and burial of a cat.

He cleared his throat. He felt uncomfortable asking Zulu about this. The lad was clearly enamoured of his human. But he was also naïve.

"Zulu, did you say that your human has a black beard?" He tried to make his voice sound casual, which appeared to work, for Zulu seemed not to detect the hostility which now exuded from George's fur.

"Yes, Sir. He does. Well, he did. But after the cat incident he cut it off. It was terrible, Sir. He loved his black beard and he had taken months to grow it. He said that now that he lived in a cosy little village, he could finally grow his beard back. He had grown up in a rough area in London you see. There was a lot of racial tension and he spent much of his life being picked on and bullied for being black. Then, when everyone went crazy over the terrorist threat, he shaved off his beard the first time. He was scared he might be arrested. Instead, he joined the police force. But he said it was such a hard job in London that he decided to move. He wanted to escape from all the drugs, crime and racial warfare that had dominated his childhood.

"When he moved here, he said he loved it – all the leafy streets, bubbling rivers and the quiet solitude. All he wanted was a peaceful life. He wanted to meet a nice girlfriend, get married and have children. He felt so safe that he decided to grow back his beard. Before he went down the pub, he'd stroke his beard proudly and then say to me, 'Zulu-mon, don't I just look like the most handsome guy in the world? Maybe tonight will be my big night and I will meet the lady of my dreams.' He was a big gentle giant, Sir, and I used to wish that he would meet someone nice because he would make a brilliant husband and father."

As Zulu paused for breath, George tossed his nose in the air. "Hmph, yes well, it all sounds very nice, Lad. But we've still got the issue of the murdered old lady, so go on with your story." Despite Zulu's commendation of his human, George was still upset. Furthermore, if the poor old woman had been murdered, then it was becoming clear that Zulu's human had a motive for that as well.

"Sir, she was no lady. She was an evil witch and after that morning, she got busy. She spread vicious lies about my human. Charlie's human can attest to that because she came to our house and told us. Apparently, the old bat was telling everyone that he was a terrorist and that he was always being visited by men with black beards in the dead of the night. Then she said she could hear my human talking to these men about making bombs and invading England. She said they all carried backpacks, so they were obviously suicide bombers.

"It was so stupid, Sir. All the neighbours actually started to believe her. That's when we started receiving death threats posted through our letterbox, telling us that if we didn't move, then we would be killed. Then someone pushed a lump of human poo

86

through the door. It was really that that broke down my human, Sir."

As Zulu rattled on in defence of his human, with an aggression he had not displayed before, he had no idea that his newest ally was fast becoming his greatest enemy. George sat there, glaring at the lad with ever increasing horror, whilst trying hard to reign in his anger and not lose track of the lad's monologue. He listened intensely as Zulu spoke of how the village people had ignored his human when he went to the shops or down to his local pub.

"Even his workmates were acting strangely towards him, Sir. The police, for God's sake!" continued Zulu, almost venomously now. "He told me that they couldn't arrest him for being a cat murderer because there was no body, but he said they still seemed affected by the old bat's comments. They knew that he was always moaning about her and that she was always ringing them to complain about me barking at her cat. But before the terrorist allegation, the police had just assumed she was mad.

"My human couldn't believe it when his workmates suddenly went all aloof and stand-off-ish with him. He said they didn't seem to care about the death threats and all the racist abuse he was getting. He was so angry and disappointed in it all. It was horrible to see him so broken, Sir. He told me that the village was obviously no different from London and full of racist bigots who were brainwashed by propaganda and who had nothing better to do than to project their own misery onto others." He slammed his bony tail onto the mud and raised his ears in anger, but if George or the other dogs had thought he was finished, they were sorely mistaken. It seemed that now Zulu had found his voice, there was no stopping him.

"On the night before the murder, he was an emotional wreck, Sir. He had cleared up the poo pushed through our letterbox, and he started to cry. Then he picked up a bottle of rum and consumed the whole lot. After that he was so drunk, he could hardly walk. Then he got abusive towards me. He told me that all this was my fault and that I had obviously killed that cat. He said he couldn't trust me and that he wished he had never got me. He even said that I was unlucky because I was black and that it was a curse to be black in this country. I couldn't tell him it was rat blood, so he really believed I murdered the cat.

"But then he went all sad again and said that I was probably provoked, as the old bat was so nasty that no doubt her cat had been too. He said he wished she would die and leave us alone."

George glanced at the other dogs. He knew they were all thinking the same as him, but he kept his jaws tightly shut. Zulu's brutal honesty would have been commendable in any other situation. However, if he had hoped to stand as a witness in defence of his human, he was hugely mistaken. Zulu rattled on though, oblivious to the fact that he was slowly but surely digging his own grave.

"It was terrible, Sir. My human was proud of his job, and he had worked hard to get it. He said that if he lost his job then we'd be too poor to afford a house and as he wouldn't be able to live in a bedsit with a dog, he'd have to give me away. He said he would rather die than be separated from me. He was crying so much that I must have licked off a pint of tears from his face." Zulu paused as he recalled the scene. His tail hung limply down behind him but as suddenly as he stopped, he started on again with a vengeance.

"When he finally stopped crying, he flew into a rage. I've never seen him so angry. He started shouting and yelling at the walls as if he wanted the whole neighbourhood to hear. He seemed convinced that the only reason everyone hated him and believed he was a cat murderer was because he had a black beard. It was so stupid, Sir. He started believing that if he shaved off his beard then that would prove his innocence. Then he marched into the kitchen and grabbed a pair of scissors. He ran to the front door, flung it open and yelled out so loudly that he must have woken up the whole street. He shouted, 'So here you go you bunch of racist bigots! Here's your fucking black beard! I hope you're happy now!' and then he got the scissors and cut off his beard."

At this point, Zulu stopped. Clearly, the thought of his human cutting off his beloved black beard in a bid to prove his innocence was too much for the lad. "It was awful, Sir. Even then, he didn't stop. He staggered out onto the street and started shouting that he wasn't a terrorist, and they could all go to hell. Then he threw bits of his beard in the street and returned back indoors to cuddle me." After telling the pack how illogical the whole thing was, and how disgusted he was with the neighbours, he finally calmed down and spoke in weary tones.

"He was really tired after all that. He crashed out on the sofa and snored all night like a bulldog. I slept with him because I was so worried that he might die in his sleep or do something stupid. I suppose I must have fallen asleep too because I never heard anything suspicious when the old bat next door was murdered."

George sighed. He had difficulty keeping his eyes open. His bones felt like they had turned to mush. He noticed the other three dogs were all slumped on their stomachs, evidently feeling the same as he. The whole thing stank as far as he was concerned. The fact that Zulu's human was so disturbed, and that he regarded his life as being destroyed by this woman, gave him a serious motive for murder. Not only that, but the whole street would now be a witness against him. Plus, he had been drunk and Zulu had let slip that he himself had fallen asleep so had not heard anything suspicious. He was about to speak, although he was not sure exactly what to say when Zulu spoke again. With a renewed level of determination and aggression, Zulu moved the story onto its conclusion, puffing away relentlessly like a little freight train heading towards a broken, concrete tunnel.

"This morning, we were awoken by the neighbours. They were standing outside our house and throwing stones at our front window. When we looked out and they saw us, they went berserk. They started screaming at us and yelling out that my human was a black murdering terrorist. They were furious, and at that point we didn't understand it. Then the police arrived and banged on our door.

"My human was terrified, so when he answered the door, he told me to stand back and wait for his instructions. He looked a complete mess, Sir. His stank of booze and still wore his white pyjamas. Plus, he hadn't shaved off his beard properly, so it sprouted out from his jaw in clumps, some long bits and some short.

"The police then told him that the old bat next door had been murdered. They said she had been shot in the chest with a gun and then she had her throat ripped out by a dog. They said the postman found her in the morning. He had gone into her house as the front door was open and there was blood on her doorstep. The police said there were splatters of blood leading right up to our door and that one of the neighbours had seen a man with a black beard coming out of the old bat's house with a dog at 5am."

As Zulu paused for breath, George sighed. He realised he could no longer describe how he felt. He wanted to believe the little dog, but all his racist beliefs were now screaming 'terrorist' and with that came the noise of the bombs exploding in the distance and Sadie, Sadie's beautiful eyes, all just a distant memory.

But before he could fold himself back into his pool of self-pity, Zulu, who seemed oblivious of George's seething mass of mixed emotions, continued, 'But it didn't make sense, Sir. My human had cut off his beard and ran into the street well before midnight, so how could he have murdered her? He was in bed asleep after that, but the police said the old bat was murdered about 4am. Plus he doesn't even own a gun so how could he have killed her?"

George tried to suppress a laugh. He scratched his head wearily and gritted his teeth. With all these constant references to black beards, guns, and terrorists, he felt like he was bordering on the edge of insanity. The little lad was relentless though and was so embroiled in his story that he seemed not to notice the incredulous and disbelieving signs from the other dogs.

"Sir," continued Zulu in full swing, "the police didn't even give my human a chance to speak. They told him that he was being arrested for the murder of Miss Lilly West and that he had the right to remain silent. When they got the handcuffs out, my human broke down in tears. He stumbled back into the hallway, and I could see the terror on his face. I just stood there, Sir. I was petrified and my beautiful human looked so sad it broke my heart."

At this, Zulu started sobbing and he had great difficulty in continuing with the story. He fell onto his stomach and sobbed into his paws but then he managed to muster up some strength again and continued, "As the police put the hand-cuffs on him he turned to me and told me to run. I didn't move so he started screaming at me, 'Run, Zulu, run!' He was so scared Sir; his eyes were nearly popping out of their sockets.

"All I wanted to do was to rip out the throats of those police and the neighbours, but I knew I wouldn't stand a chance against them all. I knew too that the only way I could save my human was to escape and then try to prove his innocence, so I ran. I flew out the dog flap and through the fence. Then I ran to our den and hid under Charlie's crate. The last thing I saw when I left the house was my human. He had fallen to his knees and was weeping."

Chapter 10

0000 hours

Zulu looked up at George as if imploring him to believe his story, but George turned his head away. He could no longer face the lad. He felt a pang of guilt for some strange reason, but he couldn't understand why. Zulu's human had clearly committed a heinous crime, black beard or not and he wished he had never become involved in this horrible affair. He wished he had stayed at home on his comfy sofa now, but it was the thought of the sofa that suddenly reminded him of the news that night – the news on TV that he had purposefully ignored. But it had obviously sunken into his mind as he had slipped back into a comforting slumber.

He vaguely remembered that the reporters had been talking about angry protests, protests that had been local and related to the possibility of terrorists in the village. The villagers had been holding a vigil outside the police station and were demanding justice. Now he realised why. It was all connected to this little dog and his beloved human who now sat in the cells.

He recalled some mention of a 'vicious dog', and that the reporters had been warning the public to steer clear of it and report the dog to the police immediately. It was then that he thought of his nightmares and flashbacks. The man out on the street last night yelling about terrorists had obviously been Zulu's human and the battle outside his house this morning had been the protest outside Zulu's house.

"It was complete mayhem," said Charlie. "Quite frankly, Inspector, I'm surprised you didn't hear it. The street was a seething mass of humans all hurling insults and throwing rotten veg at Zulu's human. Some of them were screaming for the death sentence."

Rocky perked up at this. He had an intense look in his eyes. One of voyeuristic excitement. He told the others he had been in the street that morning. "It was pretty radical. I mean the crowds were like raging. It took six coppers to drag Zulu's human out of the house. He was going mental. Shoved the cops into a brick wall and then kicked out at a reporter. He only stopped fighting when someone lobbed a tomato in his face. He seemed to give up after that. Then they shoved him into the back of a paddy wagon. A bit of a squeeze that was too, as he's so big. He just curled up into a ball on the metal floor. Like he'd lost all hope. He was crying too. Great loud, heaving sobs they were. Didn't stop the neighbours though. They were banging on the paddy wagon and trying to push it over. It took three cop cars to escort the van out of the road."

"Yes, well thank you for that vivid account, Rocky," George said with some disgust. Clearly Rocky felt like someone important, having been present at the scene and now being able to relay the sordid details to Zulu, who was already an emotional mess.

However, regardless of his contempt for Rocky, he was still reeling with the shock of it all. He couldn't believe that he had inadvertently stumbled into this mess. He had been trying hard for six months to avoid anything to do with black-bearded terrorists and now here he was, expected to seek justice for one. He realised that this was not the safe little village that his human kept ranting on about. He had been right all along. Going outside was dangerous.

He felt annoyed with his human now. Surely, she would have known about this policeman if he was their neighbour. Why hadn't she been more vigilant? She must have walked right through the battle that morning when she arrived home from work! There was no way she could have avoided it. He recalled how she had arrived home late and in a foul mood. She hadn't even told him about the suspicions about the cat, and yet she must have heard all the gossip.

He pitied the little black dog, but now he realised that his human was a suspected terrorist, his heart turned to ice. The lad was unbelievably gullible. Or maybe he was just plain stupid, for surely, Zulu would have sensed that there was something fishy about his human. George had expended all his energy defending the dog and listening to his tales of woe and all the time the silly little lad was protecting a murderer. He knew Zulu believed his own story about his human's innocence, but he was obviously so besotted with love that he had missed all the clues – clues that to George were glaringly obvious. The black, bearded giant had killed the cat and after that, he killed the old bat when he was drunk. How a dog got involved he wasn't sure. But whoever it was, no doubt it had been forced to commit the crime by Zulu's human.

He stood up to his full height and shook the mud off his fur in disgust. "Well, clearly there is no need of my assistance now. The case is obviously solved."

He turned to go, wishing he had never met these strange little dogs. They had pulled his heart in a thousand directions, but he realised he had yet more to fear if he hung about with them trying to rescue terrorists. He felt grateful they had inspired him enough to face his fear and leave his home. But now he knew there were terrorists in his midst – practically on the front doorstep for God's sake – he had no wish to stay out any longer. He had been right all along. The village was clearly a haven for black bearded terrorists running around in the guise of policemen. Why Tichfield he was not sure. However, he recalled it was near a place called Portsmouth, which was a naval port and hence surrounded by numerous navy bases. Clearly, there was a plan afoot to seize the naval base or bomb it to smithereens.

He glanced down at Zulu and then wished he hadn't. The lad looked like he had been struck by a baseball bat! George looked at Charlie perched on her throne. Her brandy eyes were as cold as frost. He felt guilty again, but he decided to stick to his guns.

"Well," he mumbled, "I really must get on then. Goodbye."

Upon hearing this, Zulu began to pace around the little den frantically. "Sir, I don't understand? You were all ears before. How can you believe my human is guilty? You can't leave now. Please, I am begging you."

George sighed. The lad's naivety was incredible. Those soft chocolate eyes looked at him imploringly. Although the desire to leave pulled at his tail, he felt he should explain. The lad deserved that much, especially after all he had been through.

"Zulu," he said gently, "your human is clearly not who you think. He is a suspected terrorist and if he is in jail then that is where he belongs."

"But sir, he's been arrested for the murder of the old bag next door and accused of killing a cat. That's hardly an act of terrorism, is it?"

"Nevertheless, he has a black beard. That's all I need to know. I've already told you that I've been fighting those mongrels in the war for eight years. They've murdered my best friends and now they've obviously moved to England." Sadie's eyes floated before him. "I have heard many a tale of terrorists hiding out in the UK ready to launch bombs and kill innocent people, Zulu, and I'm not interested. I've done my time in the war and I've no wish to go on fighting."

Charlie choked down a laugh. Sid and Rocky wagged their tails in amusement. To his annoyance, Charlie spoke. "Yes indeed, Inspector. Every day we are running for our lives. There are bombs exploding everywhere. Buildings turned to rubble." She smirked. "Evidently we are in terrible danger. I understand your fear completely."

Her sarcastic tone annoyed George, so he figured he now needed to prove his case. "So, you lot don't believe me then. Okay. Tell me this, Zulu? Has your human really been visited by black-bearded men in the dead of the night, as our neighbours have been alleging?"

Zulu looked perplexed. "Well yes, kind of, Sir. He has friends and family from London who visit all the time. But sometimes they arrive in the daytime as well."

"Well, that's suspicious enough for me, Zulu."

"But, Sir, they're good people and they all have good jobs, and some don't even have a beard. One is a barrister."

George face darkened. "A barrister? You mean he's ingratiated himself in the higher echelons of the judiciary. My God, Zulu! That is horrific news – horrific!"

"But, Sir, that's a good job. One is also a member of parliament. He has a seat in Brixton and another one, the female, well she's a teacher and she doesn't have a black beard."

George jaw plummeted to the ground. He couldn't believe his ears. "So, they are infiltrating both our parliament and our educational system. Zulu, this is not acceptable. Can't you see that there is a plan afoot to take over this country?"

"No, Sir. I thought they were all lovely people. They played with me and generally had a lot of fun. I can't see them murdering anyone, quite frankly, let alone take over a country."

"What about bombs and guns, Zulu?" said George darkly, "Did they mention any of those in between having all that fun?"

To this, Zulu actually laughed. "Of course not, Sir. I would know if they did. They don't know I understand every word they speak, so it's not as if they would not talk in front of me, is it?"

George was not convinced by Zulu's commendation of his human's friends. He knew how sneaky the Taliban were. They had mustered up a lot of power and support and they were experts at hiding out in places where others would never suspect.

"Are you sure your human doesn't have a gun, Zulu? He's a cop. He's got connections in London. How do you know he doesn't have a gun and you just haven't seen it?" George was sure the lad would be too naive to notice something like a gun.

Zulu paused to consider this. Then he raised his tail in anger. "There's absolutely no way he has a gun, Sir. He's been trained to use them obviously. But he's not allowed a gun at home and anyway, he doesn't believe in guns. In fact, he told me he hates guns because he saw too much damage done in London."

"Well, if the old bat lived next door to you, then how come you didn't hear the gun go off?" Surely the lad would have heard it. He knew he would have. He'd not miss that horrible sound.

Zulu scratched his ear and looked down at the muddy floor. After pawing the mud for a few seconds, he looked up at George. "Erm, well maybe I did hear something. I mean, sure," he shrugged, "it could have been a gun, but I was asleep, so if I heard it, I probably thought it was Sid's humans on their motorbikes.

Sometimes those bikes sound a bit like a gun and their always roaring past at odd times of the night."

George could not dispute the lad's logic. He had made the same mistake himself. Sometimes the bikes would send him ducking for cover, but other times he had just ignored them and gone back to sleep. If Zulu's human did have a gun, then where was it now? George knew the stench of a gun, but Zulu didn't. However, he was sure the lad would have woken up if his human had got up and gone next door to kill a human. Or maybe, he was so besotted by love that he did help his human? As unbelievable as that seemed, George couldn't shake off his beliefs about black bearded terrorists. He could not get his head around the idea that a man with a black beard was innocent. As he contemplated this, he saw a fly whizz past him, and he grabbed it in his jaws. As he as he absently chewed and then swallowed it, he glanced at Charlie and saw her smile.

When she spoke, it was with those same honey tones she had used before. "Inspector, as you said, flies live off excrement and those who eat them are full of verbal diarrhoea. Or should we perhaps say, shitty beliefs that have no basis in fact." She smiled again and stared through her hooded mask.

"What do you mean by that?" he growled. "My case... I mean this case is obviously proven. We're surrounded by terrorists, and we have every right to be scared."

"But is Zulu's human a terrorist, Inspector? Yes, he had a black beard, but does that make him a threat of some sort?"

George scratched impatiently at his neck. Where was this leading? He did not like this foxie's game.

She continued, "Inspector, do you realise that Zulu's human could be detained without trial, if he is deemed, in breach of the Anti-terrorist laws – laws, which don't need evidence other than a vague suspicion? Because of that rule and the poor definition

99

between the meaning of terrorist and the meaning of someone who disagrees with Government policies, now any one of our humans could be arrested or simply monitored and put under house arrest. If he is charged for terrorism, he could be in jail forever and so far, all he is guilty of, is having a black beard and friends who visit in the dead of the night. Now he's been accused of terrorism by the neighbours, the police will be spending a huge amount of time investigating his case. He could be in jail for ages." Charlie bowed her head.

George nearly exploded. He couldn't believe how much this foxy knew about human government affairs. But then he remembered how often he had listened to the news. Any dog stuck all day at home with nothing to do except think, was bound to analyse anything remotely stimulating, and the TV was considered stimulating when there was nothing else to do. He saw him doing it himself. But still. He had not seen anything resembling this law on the news or any current affair. He raised his ears in interest. "You seem to know a bit about this, Charlie?"

She flicked her tail in that dismissive manner of hers. "Inspector, my human is both an animal and human rights activist. She has a degree in law and her husband is a practising lawyer. They have both been watching the news about Zulu's human so naturally I would know of their concerns. They have been quite horrified by the reaction of the neighbours. If Zulu's human is branded a suspected terrorist, then he will have little chance of proving his innocence within the public arena. He will lose his voice, for it is unlikely that the media will represent his views.

"My humans are very passionate about free speech and that is why they state that, 'you have no free speech unless you are able to listen to those that you hate, tell their story'. When you fought in the war, did you ever sit down and listen to a man with a black beard tell his story?"

George was about to answer but Charlie remained perched on her throne and seemed determined to continue.

"In other words, Inspector, since you have only ever fought the black beards in the war, then you have no idea why they are fighting do you? These so-called terrorists do not have a voice on TV and the army and government are naturally biased?

"Maybe your enemies were freedom fighters? Maybe their lives had been destroyed by others and that is what motivated them to kill. Maybe, someone with a black beard has a serious cause for complaint or perhaps, Inspector, they are working for men with no beards or white beards, in a bid to 'stir up the pot' so to speak. The old divide and rule strategy. I mean, how do you know? Who for example benefits and who is the conqueror? Is it really your man with a black beard? Did you ever really get to hear what he had to say? Indeed Inspector, it is quite possible that the man with the black beard is nothing but a red herring."

"Red herring?" he asked.

"Yes, something that leads you astray. Distracts you from the real reason events are occurring."

George shifted on his rump. Charlie's logic slid into his heart like a cold metal blade. Like a vicious bandit brandishing an axe, she slashed at his beliefs until he felt exposed, vulnerable, and empty. Like a fish, he thought glumly, who had been gutted and then slung carelessly back into the sea. He briefly wondered what his human would make of this. It was stirring up emotions he did not want to face.

He had been told that the enemy were religious fanatics who disagreed with democracy and free speech and were therefore a threat to England. But what if the truth were that they had different reasons for fighting, but they had been banned from talking about this on the news. If that was the case, then his own country was also an enemy of democracy and free speech. If he had been prevented from hearing these people explain themselves properly, then did he really know what they were fighting about?

His human had been telling him the same thing for months. She'd perch anxiously on the edge of the sofa watching the news or some seemingly unrelated war programme and then suddenly jump up, point an accusing finger at the TV and yell, "Liars! Dirty rotten, stinking liars! Listen to this crap, George. Propaganda. Endless realms of it and people are sucking it in like there's no tomorrow! Come on you arse-holes, show us the real stuff, the story behind the scenes!"

Of course, George never paid her much attention, other than to jump every time she yelled. However, thinking about it now, he had to agree that his army had indeed done more damage to the Afghan people and their country than the Taliban had done to them. Was it any wonder that they chose to join sides with the Taliban then? As he anxiously pondered this, Charlie spoke again, and he was reminded at once of the arrogant politicians on TV.

"Perhaps one day, Inspector, the Government will tell everyone that all dogs are bad and that we should all be 'put down'. But of course, if that were to happen, we couldn't exactly tell them the true facts could we, as we would not be able to speak. In fact," she added darkly, "In order to protect ourselves, we may well have to resort to the very acts they could accuse us of. We would have to fight, would we not? We would have to resort to violence and turn on our humans or we would simply be eliminated. Without a voice, we are powerless."

Her expression was smug. George gritted his teeth. This foxy was clever but she was seriously getting under his fur. He thought about all his friends who had been killed, sometimes mercilessly by the Taliban or the insurgents in Iraq. But after that, he thought about the Taliban or really anyone with a remote resemblance to them. It was true. He had never actually sat down next to a man with a black beard nor listened to what he had to say. He was too busy fighting them.

As he sat and pondered on the possibilities, Charlie barrelled her way back into his thoughts.

"Inspector, do you also realise that even Rocky's and Sid's humans are at risk of being arrested and detained? They too have been protesting outside the police station. They're demanding the death sentence. That is why we know what they are saying about Zulu and his human."

At this, all dogs turned to Charlie. Sid growled as did Rocky. Zulu was shocked. "You mean your humans have been gunning for my blood and you've said nothing? You've not even tried to help me?" He glared at Sid and Rocky who both ignored him.

Sid growled again. "What do you mean my humans could be arrested? How so? They've done nothing wrong?"

"Well, they are holding an illegal demonstration outside the police station. According to my lawyer humans, they haven't got permission from the police, so they could be arrested too." Charlie raised her eyebrows. "Which means," she added darkly, "that all of you dogs could soon be living off the land. You would all need to learn how to hunt!" She slammed her bushy tail down on her crate. She was clearly pleased with her statement.

Sid said, "That's ridiculous, they are just sticking up for what they believe in, even if it might...be..." He glanced guiltily at Zulu, "untrue. They can't be arrested. Besides, what if they're right?"

"What indeed, Sid?" said Charlie, raising her ears. "But according to my humans, they might be wrong. Apparently, the neighbours were protesting days before the murder of the old bat, and they were protests that were based upon nothing more than rumour. Rumours started by Miss Lilly West.

"My humans were discussing whether they should hold a counter protest. They were talking about it this evening. However, when they asked the police for permission, they were told they could not protest and that if they did, then they could be accused of taking sides with a terrorist. They were told that showing any allegiance to suspected terrorists would be considered an act of terrorism as well and for that, they could be arrested."

Zulu looked perplexed. "But that can't be right, Charlie. I don't believe my human is a terrorist and I'm fighting for his freedom, but I'm not a terrorist."

"Exactly, Zulu. It's completely illogical. But it's also convenient to maintain the idea that men with black beards are terrorists, because then the government can continue on with the war with public support." She turned to George and bowed her head smugly. "Which is why I say that the black beard issue may merely be a red herring."

Sid stood up and raised his tail. "If you knew this, then why didn't you tell us?"

Charlie swayed on her throne. She seemed intent on spouting off her knowledge and gaining everyone's attention. Her tail raised up in excitement and her eyes glared through her balaclava. She glanced disdainfully at Sid.

"I didn't tell you because as far as I was concerned your humans had behaved perfectly within their rights. Of course, they should have their say, Sid. But Zulu here would disagree and sadly no one except us will ever get to hear the voice of Zulu, which is rather ironic when you consider the possible fate of his human, if indeed he does get charged with terrorism.

"Besides, even if the terrorist allegation were dropped, with regards to the murder, there is simply too much evidence against him. The murder involved a longstanding dispute, a missing cat and a trail of blood that led to Zulu's front door. It involved

104

numerous complaints, witnesses who saw suspected terrorists visiting at night and then a drunken emotional wreck of a policeman running onto the road like a crazy man. Plus, we have a witness who saw a black bearded man and a black dog leaving the old bat's house at the time of the murder. Zulu's case is a lost cause."

George had to agree with that, but he didn't want to hear any more of Charlie's monologue. His heart and mind were in the midst of a bloody battle. He wanted to race home immediately and bury his head under a pillow. He now felt as if he were suffering from shock. Not only had all his beliefs been shattered but to add to the confusion, Charlie's persona had changed completely. Instead of presenting herself as a calculating and cold-hearted psychopath, she now spoke like an intelligent philosopher with a wealth of knowledge about human rights, politics, and the human justice system. It was incredible, but maybe no more so than the information he gleaned from his human about psychology, and the endless crime movies they watched all night.

However, although she spoke keenly of human rights, he got the distinct impression she did not care about them, except to prove her point and make George and the other dogs look foolish. Her knowledge and wit were outstanding, yet her morals were clearly dubious. Plus, she still had an assertive, intimidating manner and a cold sense of logic about her. A bog-standard psychopath he could cope with, but if she were intelligent as well, then she was more dangerous than he had originally thought.

He stood up tall and said, "Exactly. How am I supposed to help? There is too much evidence against Zulu's human. I rest my case." He slammed his tail on the floor and got up to leave.

Charlie glared down at Zulu and when she did, George felt a shiver creep up his spine. He was prepared to walk out on the young dog, but what would he be leaving him with? This motley pack who seemed to have no concern for the lad. He had yet to know their whereabouts on the night the cat went missing and now there was the murdered old bat. A woman who had her throat cut open by a dog. Plus, there was a gun involved. That meant that the dog was escorted by a human. But which human, and what dog would tear out the throat of an old woman?

He glared at Charlie. What if she was just trying to confuse him? Keep him off the trail? Maybe she did know the truth and was simply covering it up? But why was she spouting off about the innocence of the black-beards and therefore Zulu's human? Why defend him, yet choose not to investigate the murder herself? She had made no effort to help the lad. At least not until he had arrived in their den. He felt his head reeling with confusion.

However, despite these thoughts, the issue of Zulu's black bearded human remained branded on his heart. He couldn't shake off his fear, nor his anger and hatred toward the bearded men who had killed all those he loved. He couldn't just accept Charlie's viewpoint without processing it first. Zulu's human had a black beard and so did some of his friends. It was time he left now and forgot about these dogs.

All this time, Zulu had been seated on the floor. He glanced with horror from one dog to the other. Suddenly he stood up proudly upon his four lanky legs.

"Sir," he said, "My human is innocent and so am I. You can't just walk away just because he has a black beard. I think the war has brainwashed you. We live in England and there is no war here. There are thousands of men with black beards in England. You can't believe that every one of them is a terrorist, surely. It's absurd. There are bad people with white skin and white beards too. How come you don't think they're terrorists when they commit murders?"

106

George shifted on his rump. "Yes, Zulu. I get your point," he snapped, although he was still unsure. His human had been telling him the same thing for months. Now Charlie was repeating it, and Zulu. But brainwashed? Him? He thought not. He was above that. Besides, he had evidence now, right here in the village. He raised his tail in aggression. He had had enough of this little black dog.

"You know what," said Zulu, his little voice now starting to rise in anger, "I think you're a racist bigot too. You are! You're no better than the neighbours and if you can judge my human without even meeting him just because he has a black beard, well, then I don't even want you on the case. You're biased, Sir."

If a bomb had landed in the middle of the den and torn them all apart with shrapnel, George would have felt relieved. Instead, the bristles on his jaw, which had become limp and lifeless over the last six months, threatened to burst from his jaw and shower this little mob with poisonous arrows. He was furious! It was all very well for him to walk off the case in disgust. At least he was leaving with his ego intact. But now the little lad was telling him to leave; telling him that he wasn't thinking logically and was therefore of no use!

He had come all this way… all this way, through the dog flap, under the fence and into this den in a bid to reassert his heroic, war-dog image and instead, he felt ridiculed, judged, ashamed and a fool. This was no hero's welcome. His medals were meaningless. And Sadie's death? What of that? If her beautiful, peace-loving, playful soul had been programmed to fight as a war dog in a war which wasn't just a lie, but one based on human greed and ignorance? What then?

His brain began to click, in a click, click, clicking frenzy as flashes of Sadie, laughing – 'the enemy can't beat us, George' – and of her tail lifting up to signify the location of a bomb; Sergeant

Jones running towards her; the click, the flash, the noise, the wind, the howl… his howl.

He started pacing around the outside of the den. He glanced at Charlie and saw her amused stare. He didn't care. He'd had enough of her patronizing, zealous attacks on his ego. He was sick of her logic because it was too logical. And although his human had been ranting on at him in a similar vein, it seemed different coming from a dog. He knew she had learned all her political and legal knowledge from listening to humans, but he did not know if she could be trusted. He did not know her agenda, her motive, and yet, he knew she had one.

He widened his pace until he was trotting further and further from the den, crashing through bushes, and paying no heed to the noise he was making. The other dogs too. They had all managed to confuse him in some way. Challenge his beliefs, change his behaviour and yet some of that had been useful. He was outside after all and it was refreshing to talk with dogs again, even if they did happen to be a horrid little bunch of characters. It was this that finally stopped him. He had been on the verge of racing back to his sofa. But knowing that he was outside again, talking to dogs who could at least understand his language, if not his actions, seemed to calm his anger, if not his continuing confusion.

As he slowed the pace and trotted around the bushes, his thoughts became clearer. Instead of thinking about the behaviour of the other dogs, he began to think about his own. He began to wonder if Zulu and Charlie were right. Certainly, there hadn't been any signs or news of any bombs going off in England. Well, a few maybe. But not enough to justify his fears.

Maybe his paranoia was taking over? He couldn't deny that his own army had bombed the smithereens out of Iraq and Afghanistan. If that were the case, then who the hell was the terrorist? Indeed, if he was a racist bigot, then he felt quite horrified. He regarded himself as a cool and objective type. However, after his last patrol, he knew all logic had left him and he knew he'd been discharged because his judgement was impaired.

Now, because of Zulu and Charlie, his deeply held beliefs were dangling precariously on the end of a tiny thread. It felt as if his whole world were about to crash. He tried to stay true to his friends in the war, yet his instinct kept telling him that Zulu was right and that maybe, black beard or not, his human really was innocent. Somehow, despite everything, he still trusted the lad.

He now realised that he would have to look at the evidence again. Take on a different perspective. The lad needed help and for some reason, he still felt compelled to help him.

He began to think about the blood. Initially he had thought it was rat blood. It was only upon hearing about the black beard that he began to take the old woman's side and consider it cat blood. Yet he had heard Zulu's story about the rat, and he believed him. If Zulu's human had not answered the door with blood on him, then the old bat would never have accused him of being a murdering terrorist.

Yet if Zulu's human wasn't a killer, then who did kill the woman, and why? Elizabeth was still missing, and they still had no idea if her disappearance was connected to the murder. There was also a witness who claimed to see a man with a black beard and a dog leave the old bat's house at 5am. Such evidence was highly incriminating, so who was this witness and if they were lying, then why?

He decided to return to the den. He sat back down and glanced at Charlie perched on her crate. Her ice brandy eyes bore into his soul. Yet again, a shiver crept down his spine. He tried to read her thoughts, but it was impossible. She was not that different from him, he thought. She had erected a concrete wall of defence around her, a wall so thick that nothing could penetrate it. But what that wall was made of, what her most deeply held beliefs consisted of, he could not tell.

As small as she was, and as different from Zulu as he was, she had still managed to smash down his defence system in one foul swoop, whilst managing to keep her own secrets intact. It was because of this, because she held so much power, and he knew deep down that Zulu was innocent, that he decided to stay.

Part two

Chapter 11

0045 hours

When George announced his decision to stay, Zulu was ecstatic. "Sir, that is wonderful news. Wonderful! My human will be so proud of you." He pranced around the den wagging his tail and then did a little jiggle and a jive in front of George. The lad's ability to forgive and forget melted the ice in George's heart. Maybe he wasn't the heroic war dog anymore, but to Zulu, he was still a hero. Still worthy of fighting for a cause and seeking justice. Still admired for his inspecting and detecting, at least by one dog anyway. He decided to put his war beliefs on hold for the duration of this case. He had a different mission now. A different dog to save and maybe, unlike Sadie, he could save him. If he left, he knew that in one way or another, the little dog would die, if not in body, then in mind and spirit.

He decided to immediately get down to business. As the four dogs stared up at him, their expressions unreadable, he outlined his plan. They would go to the old bat's house now, via Zulu's garden and through the gap in Zulu's fence. George would investigate the garden first whilst the other dogs stood back. If the murdering culprit had been in the back garden, they would have some evidence. If nothing of note could be detected, then they would enter the house.

He looked at Charlie and for once he was surprised. Her pyramid ears stood to attention and her eyes gleamed with excitement. He had expected more protests and ridicule but instead she had sat and listened, and then nodded her head to affirm her agreement with the plan.

Seeing her do this, Zulu had jumped up and barked, "Yippee," only to be bombarded with commands by the others to shut his jaws. "You're still a wanted dog, Zulu!" said George. "No need to let the whole neighbourhood know your location, Lad."

They set off, but not before George instructed them all to do one large and final toilet stop against a small tree. He had been busting for a piss throughout the whole interrogation. He noticed Charlie did a wee with one leg held up. He had to laugh. She was clearly trying to get her wee higher up on the tree to mark her dominance. It was Zulu though, who with the poise and control of a ballet dancer did a perfectly high pee, marking the tree as his, above all others. Then they all had to wait around impatiently as he did three separate poos.

"Typical," grunted Sid. "The lads always shitting himself."

When they set off, Zulu led the way, with Charlie behind him, then George, Rocky and Sid. They glided through the trees and bushes in silence, graceful yet determined, like a waft of smoke, leaving behind the burning coals of a fire. To George, it may well have been regarded as extinguished, until he heard some whispers behind him. It was Sid and Rocky. He couldn't understand their words, but they spoke to each other in frantic, worried tones. He glanced behind him, and they gave him a guilty look, then went quiet again.

George gritted his teeth and marched on. Until that moment he had been feeling proud. The dogs had listened to him, agreed with him, and they were gliding as one through the woods, as all dogs should, and all dogs can. It seemed so right and natural. They were organising themselves into a team with a mission, without need for human commands and interventions, and they were out in the wild, making full use of their senses. He could see why Zulu had such a desire to belong to a pack, even if his heart lay ultimately with his human.

He was even gaining some pleasure from this head to tail formation. From his position as third in the line, he could see Zulu's scrawny rump with his diamond triangle glistening in the moonlight and his skinny little tail held high and proud as he led the way. Charlie trotted in front of George, her tail raised in her ever-confident manner, as her plump behind wriggled away on her short, stocky legs. He had been secretly admiring her rump and had been pre-occupied with the pros and cons of the nice-bum-shame-about-the-personality conundrum, which made him snigger. He knew she would be outraged by such thoughts. He had been about to take a calculated risk and make some crude remark about her bum, just to annoy her, when he'd heard the whispers.

Now, however, he found himself thinking again, growing suspicious and negative. The two little dogs behind him were distracting him from the one bit of pleasure he'd felt all night. He was about to turn around and give them a menacing growl, when he heard Zulu say, "Okay. We're here."

Charlie stopped so suddenly, that George almost trod on her rump. As he tried to back-track, he slipped on a muddy patch of water and nearly fell on his own rump. He cursed himself for his lapse in concentration and turned to glare at the smirking jaws of Sid and Rocky.

When he turned to face the fence before them, he noticed a small gap where the fence had broken. Clearly, this was Zulu's escape route and clearly, he was not going to get through it without more sniggers from the other dogs. He sniffed the air to assure himself that there were no humans hiding out behind the fence or in Zulu's house and began to dig. As he dug, he felt his rage increase at the other dogs. He was still smarting from their comments about his weight, and he purposefully flung paw loads of mud in their faces. He heard a few bitter complaints in the background, but he refused to stop until he found himself peering once again over the top of the tunnel he had created.

Zulu's house was the same as his, except the lad's human had clearly spent more time tending the garden than his own human. The house was attached to a long line of other houses to his right, and he estimated that his own house was about six houses down. There was only one house on the left and when the other dogs appeared, he discovered that this was the house of Elizabeth and the old bat.

Zulu led him to the fence line which separated the two gardens and to the fence posts that had broken during the storm. He noticed with pleasure that there was enough room for him to squeeze through. He was still panting from the exertion of digging the tunnel. He had dug the tunnel twice as fast as he would normally, just to prove his strength. Now he was gasping for breath, so he avoided eye-contact with the others in case he saw their rotten little smirks.

When he had calmed his racing heart and lungs, he told the other dogs to stand back and await his instructions. He still brimmed with pleasure each time they obeyed him but when he peered cautiously through the gap in the fence, an ice-cold shiver crept down his spine.

The old bat's garden was a mess. The grassy lawn sprouted up in uneven clumps and the dishevelled bushes around the fence line grew ominously in towards the tiny garden, waving their bushy branches in a menacing manner. Weeds grew everywhere, threatening to take over the entire garden. Amongst all this was the awful smell of cat piss. He stared at the house. It was as dark and foreboding as the garden. Vines slunk up and across the walls, strangling the tiny house in their grip. The lights were off, but the back window, presumably to the kitchen, was open.

He sniffed again. The smell of death drifting through the window was unmistakeable. He had no doubt the police had removed the body, but they had not removed the stench of blood. They had clearly tried. George could smell something like bleach. However, his time in the war ensured he was well accustomed to the smell of blood and although it made him want to vomit, he forced himself to face it. He turned to focus on the tree beside the two fence lines. If he allowed his mind to wander, he had no way of predicting if he'd flip into a flashback.

The tree had lost its summer leaves. It stood tall above the fence and its branches poked out aggressively in all directions, as if it wielded a thousand swords and daggers and was proud of that fact. The overall effect was foul, and he now knew why Zulu hated that cat so much. Living next door to her and this horrible house and garden would have sent any good dog insane.

There was a small brick patio beneath the open window and upon that sat a table and two chairs. He also noticed the backdoor. It had a cat flap, but it was too small for him to squeeze through. Apart from the smell of death, blood, and cat piss, he couldn't smell anything else, so he decided that he had no option but to go in and investigate that garden. As per plan, he told the others to wait by the fence. He didn't want them going in and contaminating the evidence. He still had no idea if the dogs had been in there or not. If they had, he would know.

He slunk through the fence and did a slow trot around the perimeter of the garden, over the patio and then past the bushes along the back fence. He decided to avoid creeping into the bushes until he had sniffed every inch of the garden. When he had finally sniffed his way back and forth across the lawn, he was just about to tell the others to come on in, for he had not sniffed their presence when suddenly he sniffed something suspicious near the trunk of the tree. He crept cautiously towards it. The smell was offensive and again he was reminded of the war.

As he neared the offending article, he discovered that it was a piece of rotten fish, half eaten by a cat, for the smell of Elizabeth was all over it. But it was not this that reminded him of the war. The fish reeked of the smell of a drug. Except strangely, although he thought he knew the smell of every illicit drug known to man, he could not make out the smell of this one. It was not opium or cocaine. Nor was it cannabis or one of those weird new chemical drugs like ecstasy. It had only the slightest scent to it, which is perhaps why Elizabeth hadn't noticed either, for no dog and he assumed cat too, would go near a piece of food laced with a strong-smelling drug.

The others knew he had found something. They could tell by the position of his tail. It stood to attention and quivered. He glanced back at them and nearly laughed. He could see four small faces peering through the fence gap and they all looked scared. He knew they would have sniffed the smell of death and blood, and no doubt the cat piss and the ominous garden would have set their jaws on edge. Seeing their terrified faces made him feel proud. After all, it was he who had bravely entered the garden alone. He felt smug. He had not been able to explain the war to them, nor gain their empathy through words. However, now, as he looked, he saw a glimmer of respect in them, as the moon shone down into their huge brown eyes.

He ordered them onto the patio and tried to suppress yet more laughter as they each slunk in, low, careful, slow, with tails tucked tightly around their rumps. When they reached the table, they huddled together beneath it.

He wanted to yell out at them and say, "Now look who's hiding out beneath the table," but he had no time. The smell of the drug was annoying him. It could have been some form of worm tablet, yet if it wasn't, and it was a drug like opium, then he had no doubt that Elizabeth had been drugged with a fish and then taken away somewhere, either to be killed, or hidden.

Furthermore, he now knew that only a human would have used such a strategy and, in this instance, if the fish was drugged with a sedative, then he knew that the dogs were innocent.

He called Charlie over. She said she had drug experience. Maybe she knew of this one. He hadn't told her of the drug or fish but as she crept up alongside him, her small frame brushing past his hairy cloak, he saw her tail tense up with excitement as a frenzy of sniffing commenced.

"It's a drug, Charlie, but I can't detect the type," he whispered, although he was not quite sure why he spoke in secretive tones.

Charlie was not so subtle. "It's Valium," she said, in a loud, confident manner.

"Valium?" asked George. "What is Valium? Is it some kind of opium?"

"No," asserted Charlie, "but it has a similar effect. It calms a person. Makes them drowsy, floppy and uncaring about their life."

Yet again, George was impressed with Charlie's knowledge. The average fur pet would not have known that. He glanced into her eyes, and he saw that flicker of sadness again, the same one he saw when he'd first met her and asked her name.

"How do you know this, Charlie," he asked. "I thought your last human was into amphetamines."

At once her eyes turned as cold as frost. "He was," she asserted, "but when he'd been on a binge of the stuff, he needed something to calm his nerves and get to sleep. He used Valium. Wasn't into heroin he said. Didn't want to be an addict. Except he used to eat those little yellow pills by the spoonful. Like he was eating a bowl of cornflakes. Still," she paused, "he was certainly more amenable after that. Calmer, friendlier, kinder, I suppose, or maybe just too tired to be his usual nasty self."

She slammed her tail onto the grass and stared up at the full, clear moon. When she spoke again, it was in quiet weary tones. Sad tones, thought George, as he listened to her talk. "He called my smaller brother, Blow," she said. "He was a beautiful lad. Such a trusting little soul. He was generous, kind, loving and playful. I loved him like I have loved no other. But my human ruined him, Inspector. He kept spiking Blow's food with drugs. One minute he was as high as a kite on cannabis, which is why they called him Blow, I suppose, the next, he was strung up, on edge and running about like an idiot on speed. He was entertainment for my human and his mates. I tried to stop Blow from getting involved but he thought if he complied with our human, he'd be nice to us."

She glanced at George, and he saw hatred leech through her eyes as the bristles on her jaw glistened with anger. "There was only one drug my brother really liked. He was a nervous wreck in the end. His only relief was when he was stoned on Valium, same as my human. He used to beg for it. They made him beg for it," she growled. She tightened her jaws. "It made him calm. Calm enough to lay down, relax and sleep. Sometimes he would sleep for so long that I thought he would never wake up. The fact is, in

120

the end, I don't think he wanted to. He was confused and scared, yet he made out as if he was happy, just to please those drug-ridden bastards!" She spat the last word out and walked immediately to a bush to pee, and pee she did, as if she were doing her business over the sneering faces of her enemies. He had no doubt that she hated her old human and his mates as much as he hated the Taliban.

George felt a lump in his throat. He knew Charlie had experienced life, but he had not expected this. What's more, although she had clearly finished telling her story, he knew that this was just the tip of the iceberg. Yet again, as always in her presence, he felt stumped for words. He managed to mumble something akin to an apology, but it was lost on Charlie. She had exposed a part of herself to him and he knew that was all he was getting, for like his own experiences in the war, rehashing the story was all too painful. He saw the muscles on her back harden and once again, she glared through her eye-mask, as if the story she had told were nothing to her and was simply a way to explain the effects of Valium.

He decided to get back to business. He needed Charlie to have her wits about her and if she was innocent, then he needed her to focus on the present. "So, do you think this Valium could have made Elizabeth all floppy and compliant then?" he asked.

"Absolutely, Inspector. She most probably fell asleep right in the middle of eating this fish."

"But what about the yowling then? If she was asleep, she wouldn't have made a sound."

Charlie sniffed in disgust. "It's like Zulu said. She was always yowling and mewing at night. This fish probably shut her up. Enough so, that someone clearly had an opportunity to either abduct her, kill her or both. Whatever the case, her body isn't buried in this garden, or we'd find it."

George glanced at the bushes against the back fence. He had to agree with Charlie, but there was one place he had not yet investigated. As he stared at the fish, he saw something unusual from the corner of his eye. He moved up towards the bushes and inspected it. He realised that it was a human footprint. The print of a shoe or boot. Staring back at the bushes, he saw that this print had a partner and led straight into the midst of those horrible bushes. He knew he'd have to go in there but for some reason he felt scared. The bushes seemed to beckon him in, as if daring him to enter their dark, creepy nest. He knew this fear was irrational, yet he had been taught to trust his gut instinct. There was something in those bushes and unless he wanted another outburst of laughter from the others, he knew he had no choice but to go in and find out what was in there.

Chapter 12

0130 hours

George informed Charlie of his plan. He told her to go back to the table with the others and await his instructions. He felt yet another surge of triumph when she willingly agreed and noticed with glee that she slunk towards the others cautiously, her tail hanging limply behind her.

He glared back at the bushes with a renewed level of determination. If nothing else, he had yet another opportunity to prove to these dogs that he was the brave war dog after all. With his ego semi-intact, he sauntered into the bushes belying the fact that he felt as if he were entering the den of the enemy.

The bushes were thorny. They brushed up against him and hurled their thorns like vicious daggers, aiming with a precision he'd not thought possible from bushes. He remained calm though. His war training had taught him that, although God only knew what danger he faced right now. He concentrated his efforts and sniffed his way to the back fence. When he got there, he was confronted with yet another broken fence line, except this one was large enough to fit a human through. He noticed the boot prints led through the gap. Peering out to the parkland, he saw them tramp a trail towards the road.

What had happened was clear now. Elizabeth had been drugged and taken through the fence by a human. For what purpose he did not know, but there was enough evidence here to prove it, and with the trail still clear, it was possible to follow those boot prints.

He congratulated himself on his find. He was about to turn back and proudly announce his discovery when suddenly he saw something that sent a surge of pure terror down his spine. Within a split second, before he had time to freeze, he dashed out of the bushes and flew towards the table at a pace he'd not run since the war. Although the little table on the patio was a mere ten metres away, it felt like he was running in slow motion. The faster he ran, the further away the table seemed. Finally, as his legs began to turn to mush, he reached it, gasping, and panting like he'd run from the very gates of hell.

He pushed the other dogs to one side, but not without some effort. They'd seen his eyes and they'd seen his terror. They'd also been fearful about those bushes. But he had no time to gloat about their fear, for his own had clutched him in its grip and sent him right back into the war zone again. As he lay there in a quivering heap, the bombs exploded around him, and the heavy scent of smoke filled his lungs and mind once more.

How long he laid there in front of those dogs, he knew not. But when he did finally gather his wits, he realised they were whispering in frantic, worried tones. "What the hell? Jeez, he's terrified…what's in those bushes….do you think it's Elizabeth…how can he be so scared…never seen such fear…do you think he's alright? Maybe we should just go…"

It was Charlie's voice that he finally recognised. "Absolutely not, Sid. We will not run away like cowards. Look. He's coming around. Give him some space."

It was with great reluctance that George decided to open his eyes and face the pack. He was horrified. He couldn't believe how he had experienced a massive panic attack followed by a flashback in front of this motley crew. But he knew too what he'd seen in those bushes and if the others knew what he knew, if they had lived his life, then he had no doubt that they would have behaved in exactly the same manner. Regardless of that, the fear and shame leached through him as he hauled his great hairy hulk off the ground.

"Well, ha, I must say," he chuckled in an unconvincing manner, as he shook his fur down, "those bushes are quite thorny. Quite vicious little buggers, yet you'd never believe it to look at them." He coughed. "It's a good job I went in first, eh." He avoided eye contact with them. Then he wondered why he was speaking like an upper-class twat in the army. His war dog comrades would be appalled. This post-traumatic stress disorder was worse than the war itself he thought, the terror still cursing through him.

"Quit poncing around, Inspector," said Charlie. "What's in those bushes?"

The four little dogs flocked round him and stared up into his fear-ridden eyes.

"What's the go," whispered Sid in a frantic manner, "Should we do a runner or what?"

"Sir," whispered Zulu, his small black face peering up at him hopefully, "Have you found the murdering culprit? Or have you found Elizabeth?"

George tried to speak, but at first the words refused to come. When they did, he was stuttering. "It's a... it's a frigging... a frigging... oh, yuk, it's a frigging..."

He heard Charlie tut. "Oh, for God's sake, Inspector, a frigging what!"

"It' a furry... furry... a furry..."

"Furry what?" they all chimed.

"It's a furry black beard!" he yelled suddenly and turned immediately to vomit on the ground.

"A what?" demanded Charlie. "Have you uncovered a human dead body or something?"

As George began to gather his wits, he realised that if it had been a dead body, he'd have been relieved. He stared up at the moon and thought of his sofa and his cupboard under the stairs. The desire to race back home tucked at his tail. He felt irritated now. Irritated that this little lot would never understand him. "It's a frigging, beard. A fake black beard, I think. One like my human wears." He spat. "One like the thousands of Taliban men I killed in the war," he added with a growl.

"You mean like one of those things you get in a shop?" added Sid, who looked as if he was about to laugh.

"Yes! One of those," he growled. To his horror, the four little dogs burst out laughing. He could see they had been trying hard to reign it in, out of politeness he assumed, but he knew too that their fear, followed by the relief that there was no actual danger, was all too much. Hysteria would be next he thought glumly. Hysterical laughter, which is exactly what happened, so he trotted away angrily to sit by the fence.

If he had hoped that time would cure them of their laughter, he was sorely mistaken. With great bravado, one which he had not seen before in this garden, he saw Rocky dash into the bushes and race back triumphantly, holding the dreaded black beard in his

126

jaws. As more laughter commenced, George decided that he'd had enough. He was going home. This lot could solve their own pathetic murder he thought, and he got up at once and padded over to the gap in Zulu's fence.

Immediately he felt a presence beside him. The laughter had been reduced to quiet snickers and chortles, and he knew, without looking, that it was Zulu beside him.

"Sir," he whispered, "We're sorry. Really, we are. Please don't go. You've helped me so much. You can't leave now."

George knew he was sulking, but he couldn't shake off the shame. He refused to answer and instead increased his walk into a purposeful trot. As the gap in the fence grew nearer, he heard Zulu yell, "Sir. You can't leave me now. I need you. Please. You're braver than all of us put together. Look what you've done already. Please! Don't go."

George felt sure the lad was about to cry. That was the next part of hysteria. Bawling one's eyes out at the imagined horror that had never occurred but could have.

For Zulu though, the horror wasn't the beard and the seemingly absurdity of George's fear. It was the loss of his newest ally. His friend, his hero in all this. The one who had taken the time to help him. It was himself. Sergeant George Penkins. K-nine specialist in bombs, guns, and drugs.

George knew this intuitively, which is why he decided to yank his head in and push his sulking ego aside. Once again, he felt Zulu pulling him back. Challenging him to more of this horrific scenario. All he had wanted initially was to rush out the dog flap, tear apart the dogs and then return home. Instead, he was faced with the appalling idea of protecting a suspected terrorist, and perhaps a murderer, who had no qualms about utilising a fake black beard to achieve his goal. The goal of murder, which Zulu was reliant on him resolving.

With a great sigh, he stopped and turned back towards the others. They had recovered from their hysteria now and for once they were subdued.

The fake black beard sat under the table, the dogs standing back as if it were now a threat of some sort. George trotted slowly towards it. As he did so, Sid spoke. "Inspector, is this the same sort of beard that your human wears in the car when she sits in the driveway and tries to calm you down?"

George felt an urgent need to attack the dog and return home, but he stuck to his guns. "Indeed, it is, Sid," he said, as he grew nearer to the offending article. "In fact, it is exactly the same as my human's fake beard." As he sniffed his way cautiously towards it, Sid interrupted his thoughts. "Inspector, do you not think it a tad suspicious that a fake black beard, one like your human wears, is here, in the midst of a bloody murder scene?"

George stopped as he considered this. When he looked up at the other dogs, he saw their faces darken with suspicion. Even Zulu's face had taken on a harder look. Sid shifted on his rump and shrugged. "I mean, even my humans have been saying she's a bit of a nutter. Like, no offence, Sir, but she is kind of out there and she does seem to like wearing those fake black beards. It's a bit weird that one of her black beards turns up in the bushes, hey." He shrugged, again in a casual manner. "I mean." He coughed. "I'm just saying it, is all. Like, putting it out there as a possibility, like." Again, he shrugged.

"Putting what out there as a possibility, Sid?" George growled.

Sid just sat and stared at him. As did the others. Four pair of eyes that now looked up accusingly, as if he himself had murdered the cat. "Is this a joke?" he said. "Do you think that after all my time in the war I wouldn't have known if I was living with a murdering psychopath?"

Again, the dogs remained silent. As his stomach did a double flip followed by a single roll and a triple tumble, he sensed a growing level of aggression from the other dogs. As they glared up at him, he felt his heart sink.

He couldn't believe it! If his human was the murdering culprit, then what kind of fool was he? He knew she was obsessed with killers. She was always studying the psychological profiles of murderers or watching horror movies on TV. Maybe she really was unhinged. Maybe she had been so damaged by the war that she had lost her ability to be a law-abiding citizen? Certainly, she was fighting her own internal war.

Maybe all this therapy and training was some kind of sick joke that she could play out so she could dress up like the terrorists she'd been fighting? Even he had begun to suspect that her intent to cure him was due to her own misery, more than his own.

Now, the more he thought about it, the more he realised that a human running around dressed in a black beard with a towel on her head was a bit mad. Or maybe, just maybe, she was seriously deranged? But it was completely illogical. He knew that. Deep inside he knew. His human was kind. Compassionate. Mixed up from the war maybe, but she was no murderer, not of a cat and certainly not of an old lady. He would know, wouldn't he?

As he contemplated all this, he saw a small black face invade his visual field. It was Zulu and he was not happy.

"So," Zulu yelled, "All this time I've been trusting you and putting up with you doubting me and my human and all this time it's been your human who murdered the old bat! I can't believe it!" He slammed his bony tail on the patio. "You've more or less told me I'm stupid, and all this time it's you who has been the idiot. You, who has been living with a murderer!"

George felt horrified. This surely could not be happening, but before he could say anything, Charlie charged in with her own accusations. "So, Inspector, it looks like the evidence is stacking up against you. Exactly where is your human tonight, and where was she last night, for that matter?"

George coughed and glanced away. He felt guilty for some reason, but he couldn't explain why. "Erm, well, she was at work all night, wasn't she," he said, and then snarled. "She was at the hospital saving lives not killing people!" he slammed his tail down on the patio to emphasize his point, but it did nothing to stop the tide of suspicion hurtling his way.

Zulu glared at him. "So, Inspector," he snapped with an aggression he'd not displayed before, "Does your human go to work at night with a backpack on her shoulders?"

George cleared his throat. "Well actually, Son, she does. But it's to carry her dinner and her other work stuff," he spat. "If she had a bomb or weapon in it, I'd know wouldn't I. I mean, that's my area of expertise, isn't it? Besides, what has a backpack got to do with this murder?"

The four dogs looked doubtful. Rocky intervened. "Inspector. As you said before. We might be dealing with a crazy, murdering terrorist. You kept asking Zulu about his human friends and their backpacks, so why can't we ask you the same questions?"

George gritted his teeth.

Sid charged in with his own question then. "Inspector, if your human was in the army, does she own a gun?"

George's heart sank. With a growing horror he realised that his human did own a gun. One which she kept in her bedside drawer and which she insisted she needed for protection. He'd only seen it once. She'd been drunk and had staggered out of her bedroom wagging it in all directions. George had been asleep on the sofa at the time. When he awoke and saw her, he was so scared that he froze.

As he watched her dance around the tiny lounge yelling out, 'Take this, you murdering swine' and 'Yeah, right, you bastard, you think you can take me on?' he recalled feeling damn queasy. But then she'd turned to him and laughed. 'Don't worry, George. You're safe with me. If any enemy attacks us, hiccup, they'll be dead meat,' and she'd marched back into her bedroom, gun aimed at some non-existent enemy.

When he admitted his human did have a gun, Zulu was livid. "If your human has a gun, inspector, then how do we know she's not a murdering terrorist? She goes out at night. She wears a backpack. She has a stash of fake black beards. Now you say she owns a gun. All this time you've been calling my human a terrorist and it's your human who is the mad one. Your human who must have killed the old bat and let my human take the blame! I hate you. I hate you!"

As the lad lunged towards George, he saw the killer flash of white teeth. Within a second, before he'd had time to consider the change in Zulu's pleasant, soft demeanour, he forced his right paw down on Zulu's neck and twisted him onto his back. With the lad now under him, thrashing and barking away like a maniac, he bent down towards the young dog's throat and snarled, "Lad, if my human was responsible for your human's fate, and if indeed she is the killer, then I will have no hesitation in ripping out her throat!"

Charlie strutted towards George and demanded he relinquish his grip on Zulu. She then announced that there was only one way to prove either the guilt or innocence of George's human. "We need to sniff it," she said, referring to the black beard. "If the murderer or culprit was wearing that beard, then we will know..." She cleared her throat. "if it was the Inspector's human or not."

George decided that as he had found the beard, it should be he who examined it. He had no desire to go anywhere near the rotten thing, but he felt that as his human was now under suspicion, it should be he who proved it either way. The others were not convinced.

"Oh, for God's sake," he snarled, "you can all have your sniff after me if you want. It's not as if I can hide the evidence now is it. I tell you all now, if my human is a murderer, I'll kill her myself and be damned about the consequences." He smashed his tail onto the patio as the others backed away. When they did so, he realised his mistake. The last time he'd had his jaws buried in a beard was when he attacked that fake beard his human used and that had led to a panic attack. Before that, he'd had his jaws clamped down on the furry neck of a Taliban insurgent, who'd tried to escape when he'd found weapons in the man's house.

His agitation rose but he knew he could not back down. A murderer had been seen coming out of the old bat's house and that murderer had been wearing a black beard. If the beard was indeed a fake, a red herring as Charlie called it, then George had no doubt that the murderer's stench would be scuttling around in the furry mass of that dreadful beard.

He stood back, braced himself and told the others to stand clear. He took a few deep breaths to calm his racing heart and then crept down low, sniffing cautiously towards the beard. As he moved nearer, he got the slight scent of human on it. A frenzy of sniffing commenced as he came up close to the beard. As his nose focused exclusively on the task at hand, he forgot his fear of the beard. He forgot because almost immediately, he knew who the murdering culprit, or at least, Elizabeth's abductor, had been.

Chapter 13

0215 hours

It was obvious to the others that George had discovered the culprit. They simply read the signs. George's tail stiffened to attention and the hackles on his back rose like a million soldiers ready for battle. This was followed by a low growl, an angry bark, and then surprisingly a frenzy of tail wagging followed by a quick, bouncy trot around the garden. When he finally sat down his expression was smug.

"Well, I take it it's not your human then," snapped Charlie. "So come on, who is it?"

George began to chuckle.

"Sir! Why are you laughing? This is serious. Who's the murderer? Who took Elizabeth?" demanded Zulu, whose small black face seemed to grow darker by the second.

"Son, Son I apologise," chuckled George. "It's just that now I've got the sniff of him, it's so blindingly obvious that I wish I had thought of it before, that's all."

133

"So, it's a him then? Are you going to enlighten us further, Inspector or should we just get on with the business of sniffing it ourselves?" Charlie was clearly impatient, and he had no doubt that she hated being kept in the dark.

He paused for as long as he could, before announcing proudly, "My friends, it is definitely not my human who was wearing that beard, but," another pause, "he has indeed met my human and he did specifically enquire where she purchased her beard."

"And," snapped Zulu, who was also growing impatient.

"And my friend, the culprit we seek is in fact..." He paused again for dramatic effect. "... our very own local postman!" He slammed his bushy tail onto the patio and growled, "It's the very same postie who comes to our houses everyday with our mail and who probably knows every damn thing about us. The same postie, no doubt, who conveniently found the old bat dead first thing this morning."

He stood over their surprised faces and enjoyed the moment. His ears rose triumphantly as he told them how he knew this and when he had first met the postie face to face. He explained that his human had arrived back from work in a cheerful mood one morning. "It was about three months ago," he asserted. He then told them that his human got drunk on a bottle of booze. "She had two days off," he explained, "so she was happy and keen to get drunk, but sadly, for me, that meant more training with the black beard." He told them she had gone to her bedroom to get ready but before she emerged, the doorbell had rung. It was the postman. When she answered the door, she was so drunk she forgot that she was wearing her nurse's dress, along with a white tea towel on her head and a fake black beard."

He recalled that the postie had been somewhat confused and had apologised profusely saying that he thought he was delivering a parcel to a Miss P. Jones but evidently, it was for a Mr P. Jones.

He had watched his human laugh with embarrassment as she realised her error. Then, in one dramatic gesture, she had torn off the beard and told the postman that she was actually a Miss and that she had simply been preparing for a fancy-dress party.

George told them how a grin of admiration had crept up the postie's face, as he slowly looked her up and down. His human was too drunk to notice, though. The postie had then asked where she had got such a realistic beard. She had told him that it was from the internet, a site called www.islam-is-us.co. He had then passed her the parcel, but his hand had lingered too long on his human's arm, so George had got off the carpet and padded towards him snarling.

The postie had backed away, smiling, and still eyeing up his human. "He had an evil, cunning look about him, that postie. I wouldn't put murder past him, that's for sure. And he had a short beard. It was white though, not black, and he was pale and thin. Damnit," he growled, "I wouldn't forget the smell of that snivelling creep."

"By God, I knew there was something fishy about that postman," snarled Charlie.

"Yeah, he always gave me the jitters," added Rocky, "I've given his hand a few little nips through the letterbox in my time."

"Me too," chimed Zulu. "I can't believe it, Inspector; you've solved the case. My human can be freed at last." Suddenly he barked out a loud "yippee" and then jiggled and jived around at a dizzying pace.

"Son, Son. I think you should calm down. We haven't exactly found the murderer yet. He might be connected, but so far, all we may have is the abductor and the possible killer of Elizabeth. We've got a fish, a few boot prints, and a beard," said George, "But I have to admit, given that he's taken to wearing fake black beards and drugging cats, it does make him a very strong suspect.

The witness said she saw a man with a black beard leaving the old bat's house, maybe it was him, wearing a fake black beard and for some strange reason, making some attempt to set up your human."

"That's true," spoke Charlie, "but what about motive. Why would the postie take a cat and then murder the old bat, and what would he have against Zulu's human?"

All this time, Sid had been sitting in silence with a strange, evasive look in his eye. This hadn't gone unnoticed by George. In fact, he could distinctly smell fear emitting from the dog's fur.

"So, what's your opinion on this, Sid," he asked, "You've not had a word to say about it. Do you want to sniff the beard and confirm it's the postie or what?"

Sid walked over to the beard and had a sniff. When he returned, he denied it was the postie. But he couldn't look George in the eye when he said it, and he spoke with a nervous tremor. The other dogs decided to have a sniff too. They could all see Sid was acting weird, but after sniffing the beard, Charlie and Zulu were fully convinced it was the posties scent all over it. Rocky however, gave Sid a wary look and then told the others that he wasn't so sure.

"Well, that's three against one and a possible half, Sid," said George. "Are you going to doubt the noses on all of us?"

Sid flattened his ears, and his tail grew limp. He sat down and sighed. "Oh well, it's a bit awkward, all this. I mean, if I tell you what I know then you're immediately going to suspect my humans and probably me, but I know I'm innocent and so are my humans."

"Well, Sid. I guess that then makes you a fully-fledged member of the which-one-of-us-did-it club then," snapped George. "Come on now. Look alive. We've all done our confessions. We've all been accused. You may as well spit it out."

Finally, Sid managed to speak. He told them how the postie had been a regular visitor at his house. "He is always delivering parcels," he said.

"What kind of parcels?" demanded Charlie.

"Erm, well the kind that contains bags full of drugs, I suppose." Sid shrugged as the shame leached through him.

"Drugs," snapped Charlie, "are you telling me your lot have been involved in drug deals? I knew it!" She slammed her tail onto the patio. "Every time you turn up at the den you look half cut – eyes glazed. For God's sake, Sid, you can't even remember your own name half the time. What the hell are your humans into? Are they drugging you?"

"No, no." Sid coughed. "It's not like they're drugging me. It's just that they smoke so much of the stuff that I can't avoid breathing it in. It's only hash, I think. They make up really big joints."

George was beginning to feel sorry for Sid. The dog was clearly embarrassed, yet George felt that Sid was holding something back. There was more to this than just drug deliveries and drug deals. "What else, Sid? "he said, "There's something you're not telling us."

"Um, well again, I feel kind of awkward like, erm..."

"Just get on with it, Sid," yelled Charlie, who's irritation with Sid was evident.

"Well, this is the part where you're going to hate me but oh well, here goes. On the morning of the murder, me and my humans had arrived back from an all-night festival in the woods. We got home about 6am. When we did, the phone rang. I don't know who it was but when my human put down the phone, he told the others that he'd been told he had to return a favour." Sid began pawing slowly on the ground. "I mean, it was a lie, just a little lie, but all the same..." He scratched his ear. "it did kind of point the finger at Zulu's human."

Zulu's tail grew tense. The lad was glaring at Sid.

"Go on," said George, "What favour, what lie?"

"Well, the favour required that my humans tell both the neighbours and police that they saw a black bearded man leave the old bat's house around 5am. They were supposed to say that the man had a dog and walked straight up Zulu's driveway to his front door."

Before Sid had a chance to raise his head, a flash of black smashed into him, white killer teeth gleaming like daggers. Zulu's anger had turned to rage. The attack on Sid was a frenzied one. Sid was on his back one minute, beneath the gnashing jaws of Zulu, the next, he was chasing Zulu round the garden trying to twist him onto his back. As the snarling increased, the look of hatred on the dogs' faces intensified. They seemed equally matched, their kicks and wrestles too fast to keep track of. One minute it seemed that Zulu was the winner, the next, Sid.

"Charlie," asked George, "do you think we should stop them. I mean Zulu is out for blood now and Sid is no angel. What if they kill each other?"

"That will not happen, Inspector. I've taught them well. Killing other dogs, especially pack members, is simply not allowed. Besides," she said, "it's time Zulu fought his battle. This has been long overdue. He has a talent for fighting, but he lacks the emotional intensity to drive it. This will help him learn more, I think."

George tutted. He was sure the lad could fight. He had fought off three dogs in the past. But getting emotions tangled up in fights were not safe as far as he was concerned. It could lead to fatalities, and he could not understand why Charlie needed the lad to hate. Stand up for himself yes, but not hate.

As it was, Sid finally gave in. He was lying beneath the snarling jaws of Zulu, and he was clearly knackered. Zulu smashed his tail down on the neck of Sid and walked back to the others, a disgusted look now written all over his face. He was still panting as he arrived to sit with the others.

"Well done, Zulu," said Charlie, "You did well, with an aggression I've not seen before, but you maintained control."

"Control," panted Zulu, "I should have killed that lying piece of scum." He regained his breath and snarled, "So now I know why he didn't want to help me. All this time the cheating little bastard was covering for his humans! He was even prepared to see me put down for murder."

"But you didn't kill him, did you Zulu and you know why," said Charlie.

Zulu scratched his ear and appeared thoughtful. "Well, it's not because I'm supposed to be a runt," he snapped suddenly, "and it's not because he's a pack member. I could have ripped out his throat in a second if I'd wanted but I didn't, because…"

"Because of what, Zulu?" asked George. He was sure that if he had been Zulu, he would have killed Sid, so he was curious now. A part of him felt sad for he could see that Zulu's sweet innocence was sliding away like huge chunks of snow in an avalanche, yet still, he had not killed. Was it really because of Charlie?

"I suppose I didn't kill him because he was protecting his humans and I don't know if I would have done the same or not. If Sid's humans get arrested, then he'll have no home either and he'd be at risk of going to the dog pound and being put down. I hate him for what he did, but I understand it."

Charlie tutted. "Zulu. When I said don't kill other dogs because of other humans, I didn't mean that you don't kill if that dog was prepared to let you die. You've still not understood. You're thinking too much about the other humans or dogs, which is exactly like a runt, if you don't mind me saying. If your life is at risk and it was their fault, then you should at least spill some blood."

George thought that sounded hypocritical after her big speech about pack members, however as she finished, Sid arrived to sit with them. He was limping and he looked a muddied, scuffed up mess. He was still panting from the exertion of the fight, but he managed to speak, "He did spill blood, Charlie. Look." He turned and showed them his back thigh. It was covered in blood and seeped out from an open gash that was clearly caused by a pair of dog's jaws.

George noticed that Charlie looked impressed. When he turned to Zulu, he saw that the lad was brimming with pride. He tried to suppress a laugh. He was glad Zulu had shed some blood. Sid deserved it, but he was also glad that Zulu had maintained some of his principles and enough logic not to go in for the kill.

"Lad," he said, "I'm very proud of you. Being able to fight and cause injury to the enemy is what we seek in the army. Killing is a last resort. You did well, Son, and I'm not sure I'd have managed to be so controlled if I had been you." He slapped his bushy tail onto Zulu's back as if to congratulate him.

"Well, I guess that makes Zulu the winner then," said Charlie. "I agree, you did well. You've clearly learnt much from my training. I just hope that those kind thoughts of yours don't interfere with your hunting in the future."

"Oh, give the dog a break, Charlie," snapped George, "Why do you have to refer to his supposed failings when he's just won a fight? What is it with you?"

Charlie shrugged and turned away. Staring up at the moon she mumbled, "I just don't want him to be a people-pleaser, dog-pleaser or whatever, Inspector. If Zulu keeps thinking about other animals, who either harm him or whom he needs to hunt and kill, then he won't survive on this earth, that's all." Then she turned to George and snarled, "To beat the enemy you have to think and behave like the enemy. You can't afford to be nice."

140

As she glared menacingly through her balaclava, George finally realised he'd found her soft spot. Her trigger point. That vulnerable part that made her act like a bitch. It was clear that she recognised the same qualities in Zulu as in her brother. Blow had been a naïve, sweet little people-pleaser and probably a runt too. But he'd lost his spirit and his mind to the drug baron by attempting to be nice. It all made sense now. She wanted Zulu to hate, to be angry and feel as if he had a right to be so. By doing that, then Charlie clearly thought the lad would be better able to survive. Her agenda was to protect the lad and she was doing it the only way she knew, using brutal bully tactics to provoke hatred from the lad.

He was about to speak and tell her she had it all wrong when Rocky suddenly spoke. He looked somewhat impatient. "Well, what now then? Are we going after the postie or what? Clearly, he's the murderer. Sid's lot are innocent of murder because they were at a festival. Are we just going to stand here all night talking or what?"

"Just hold on, Rocky," snapped George, who had no doubt that Rocky was annoyed that Sid had lost the fight. "We've got a few more facts to establish here and it seems that Sid has the answers to some of them." He glared at Sid who shifted uncomfortably on his rump. "So, Sid, are you now telling us that your humans are drug dealers?"

Sid coughed and scratched his ear. "Erm, well, I suppose so. Only small-time stuff though. Just like to friends and neighbours and only a bit of hash." He glanced at Charlie with a guilty look. "Erm, and maybe a bit of that white stuff they call 'speed'." He shrugged and began pawing at the patio. "I mean it's not my fault is it," he said glumly, "It wasn't me who asked them to sell it was it, but it was definitely that postman who did the deliveries. He didn't say much, and he never hung around. He just took their money and disappeared. Up the road like, to deliver the mail."

"What else, Sid," demanded George, "What else do you know?"

Sid shrugged helplessly. "Well, I admit that my humans weren't too chuffed about a copper living nearly opposite them. They were always moaning about him and wishing he'd move. Slowed down business, they said, and they didn't want to get caught. When all that stuff happened with the neighbours and the old bat's cat, they said it was damned convenient and that they hoped the big black copper would move."

"I suppose they put the death threats and the human poo through our letterbox then," snapped Zulu.

Sid gave a tiny tremor of fear and then glanced down at his bloody thigh. "Err, well, they did, err, participate in that Zulu, yes, I admit. But," he added defensively, "It was that postman who delivered the death threats my humans wrote. It was his idea actually. He told my humans to get busy and get nasty. The whole plan was to get rid of the cop. They thought he would leave the neighbourhood if they gave him enough jip."

Charlie turned to glare at George. Her expression was smug. "So, Inspector, it seems I was right after-all. Your black beard is nothing but a red herring."

George scratched an ear with his paw. Why was she bringing this up now? He thought they were over that argument. Clearly Charlie couldn't let sleeping dogs lie. "What are you going on about now Charlie and why bring up all that?"

"Because, Inspector, now we know this whole sordid affair is related to drugs, we've got a mission on our hands. The postie is probably just a drug runner, just like your Taliban black-beards in the war. The real culprit, the true enemy, always remains hidden.

A clever tactic, which makes our job that much harder. I doubt we'll ever find the murdering mongrel now."

"What do you mean," demanded George, "We've got our suspect and what's all this got to do with the war anyway?"

"My humans say Afghanistan is the biggest manufacturer and dealer of opium and hash on this Earth. Do you really think that the true owners of the land and of course the drugs, would parade around conspicuously with black beards? No, Inspector. People blame black-bearded Taliban's for dealing drugs, but that's just a clever way to distract us from the truth."

George sighed and stared up at the stars. "And what truth is that, Charlie? What truth is it that really gets up your frigging arse?"

Charlie sniffed. "What gets me, Inspector, are the lies and the fact that the real enemy never gets caught, because people are so dumb and stupid. Even dogs," she added darkly. "When I lived with my drug baron, he didn't deliver the drugs himself. He got me and Blow to do it while he waited up the road in his car. We'd carry the drugs in our collars or on our backs and exchange the drugs for money. If Blow and I got caught, well what could we do? We couldn't exactly tell the police who the true culprit was, could we. Because we wouldn't have a voice.

"Just like your Taliban who are accused of terrorism and don't have a voice. It was a clever manoeuvre on the part of my drug baron, Inspector, and I've no doubt that the drug barons who control the opium in Afghanistan will remain as undetected as he did. That is why I say that knowing that the postie runs drugs, does not mean we have our true culprit. A drug runner is not necessarily a murderer. That, Inspector, is my point," she snapped.

"Well, it's a very long point," said George who was growing impatient. "But you've made it now and we've got a job to do here.

This postie may be a drug running red herring, but it's a start, isn't it and it's time we got on with the business of solving this case."

"I agree, Inspector," asserted Zulu, "But what I don't get is the part about Elizabeth? Why take her? It was a complete accident that the old bat thought me and my human were suspects. So, stealing a cat in the hopes that the old bat would blame my human and cause a big fuss – enough fuss to make my human want to kill her – is a bit farfetched don't you think?"

Before George could speak, Charlie, who seemed not at all put out by being shifted out of the conversation, barrelled her way back in. "It's not that farfetched if you consider that we're up against a very clever enemy now. Someone who owns a gun and who will do anything for money. Planning ahead is not unusual if you want to commit murder and get away with it."

"It might be something really simple though," said George, "The cat got taken and killed because the old bat owed the drug dealers money, so it was pay up or else. Maybe she didn't pay up, so they shot her and left Zulu's human to take the blame."

"Yeah, but I don't ever recall the old bat coming to our house," said Sid, "and my humans never mentioned her taking drugs."

"She always stank of alcohol when she came to our place to complain," said Zulu, "but she was crazy. Maybe the postie delivered her the drugs."

"Well," said George, as he turned towards the creepy little house, "I guess there's only one way to find out. If the murdering culprit was not the postie, then we shall know, won't we! We will simply sniff him," he paused, "or her, in that house."

Chapter 14

0300 hours

The four dogs turned as one and stared up at the house. It rose above them, like a hostile enemy ready to attack. Once again, they were assaulted by the smell of death, although George had enough wits about him to notice that it drifted out through the open window. He glanced at the tiny cat flap to confirm his suspicions. He would not get through that cat flap, but he could get through the window.

He thought about the complexities of the case. The postman was still a suspect but, despite the fact that the dogs now seemed innocent in the whole affair, there was still the case of the mysterious dog. The one who had buried its jaws in the throat of the old woman.

His inspecting skills had taught him to remain ever vigilant and always suspicious. The dogs seemed innocent but what if they weren't. If they all went in at once, then they'd contaminate the evidence. He had no doubt that the forensic police had already scoured the place, but he knew, at least from the TV, that investigations were never complete. If Zulu went in for example, then he'd leave evidence which would go against him in a court of law. He couldn't exactly tell Zulu to wear a plastic outfit to prevent his fur dropping off onto the floor.

He thought hard. He saw Zulu scratch impatiently. "I don't think you should go in, Son," he finally said, turning to Zulu. "In fact, I don't think any of you should go in."

At first the others looked shocked. Then their looks turned to suspicion.

"Why not, Inspector?" said Sid, who had clearly regained some of his composure now his horrid little secret was out. "The postie might be our target, but your human is certainly no angel. Maybe you don't want us sniffing out the smell of a female?"

"Damn you, Sid," growled George, "I'm only saying this to protect you." He knew that was only a partial truth. "If you lot go in there dropping your fur all over the place then the cops will have a field day. You are aware of DNA, aren't you?"

The dogs were not, of course, although he was surprised by Charlie's lack of knowledge if her humans were lawyers. He only knew about DNA from the TV and the hundreds of episodes of crime programmes he watched with his human. He briefly explained about connecting suspects to the bodily evidence they left behind at a crime scene. When he did, the others understood. "We dogs are probably a lot better at discovering culprits because we have the use of our nose. But humans have to go through a lot of trouble to find out the same thing. The end result is the same though."

"Ah yes, that's true, Inspector," chuckled Charlie, "My humans always say that they'd be better able to prove the guilt of someone in a case if a dog could talk. They reckon that if you put a dog at a crime scene and then as a witness in court there would be no need of a jury. It'd make their jobs easier, they told me. They often said that a lie detector would be better run by a dog." She wagged her tail, clearly pleased with the fact that yet again, she could prove how pathetically weak and useless humans were.

Although George was starting to get some understanding of Charlie's hardened character, her bitterness towards humans was relentless. She was more damaged than him he thought, and he'd fought a God damn war.

Before he could contemplate this further an angry black face appeared below him. It was Zulu and his chocolate eyes were as dark as coal. "Inspector, if you think I give a flying toss about DNA and all that rubbish then you're sorely mistaken." The bristles on his face quivered and his jaw was as hard as steel. "I am not hanging around here listening to anymore of you and Charlie's intellectual claptrap. I am going in that house, and I am going in now!"

With tail held high and proud, Zulu raced to the back door and hurled himself through the cat flap with a loud smash. As the three dogs stared at the door in horror, the cat flap swung back and forth with a vengeance, rattling, and squeaking away in the silence. As it slowed to a final halt, Zulu's face poked out. His bravado had clearly diminished but despite his fear, he was still angry. "Are you lot coming," he said, "or are you going to stand there like a bunch of gossiping cowards?"

George had no time to outline his plan, nor any time to insist that the dogs remain outside. With Charlie in front, the three small dogs raced to the cat flap and entered the house with another three resounding crashes. No one wanted to be accused of being a coward it seemed, and George found himself outside, alone, and severely irritated that they'd disobeyed his orders. However, now a decision was made, he realised he'd have to clamber up onto the table and get in that house via the window. When four small faces peeked out from the cat flap, they saw his great hairy hulk standing precariously on the tiny table as it wobbled under his weight.

The window was easy to open. It had an old-fashioned latch which lifted off its hinge leaving George to swing the window open and enter the house. It was the kitchen window so when he heaved himself through it, he found he was perched uncomfortably over the kitchen sink. Immediately he resisted the urge to vomit. The sink was stacked high with mouldy crockery and was full of blackened water from the mould. A flurry of flies flew up at him, like vicious army jets ready to attack.

He realised he couldn't attack back for any sudden movement would disturb the mountain of rubbish on the kitchen sideboard. If he shifted position, the whole lot would go hurtling down onto the tiled floor, making a loud smash. He had wanted to enter the house silently, like in the war, which is why he was so furious with the other dogs for smashing their way through the cat flap. He stood there carefully as he observed his surroundings.

The kitchen was disgusting. Used tin cans of baked beans and cat food lay scattered across the worktop. In between these, lay numerous empty vodka bottles. George recognised the smell. It was the same poisonous substance his own human drank, although she tended to clean up after herself. A few ashtrays sat amongst the mess – their bowls full to maximum capacity with stinking cigarette butts. Further along, a huge pile of newspapers and shredded mail threatened to topple over onto the tiled floor.

George looked down. He'd have to move carefully. If he jumped and this lot smashed to the floor, he'd wake up the whole neighbourhood. As he calculated his next move, one paw here, another placed there, he saw Zulu enter the kitchen. Before he'd had time to tell the lad to be quiet, Zulu barked, "Yippee, He's made it!" and suddenly George slipped on the mouldy, wet worktop and fell.

148

He landed hard, hard enough to wind him, but not hard enough to distract him from the sound of the crockery, glasses, bottles, tins, and ashtrays smash down beside him and onto his back. Laying in the pile of rubbish and now stinking of booze and cigarette ash, he looked up at Zulu and growled, "Well done, Son, well done!"

Zulu seemed oblivious to George's anger. As he hauled himself up from the great mound of clutter, and placed his paws carefully in between the broken glass, Zulu pranced around in front of him. Jiggling and jiving away, tail wagging furiously, he yelled, "Sir, Sir, we've found the body. We've found out where the old bat died."

George realised the lad was buzzing out on adrenaline. It took a lot of courage to race through that cat flap and it was clear that he was feeling euphoric and victorious. As the three other dogs arrived at the kitchen doorway, their looks a mixture of fear and excitement, he gritted his teeth.

He wanted to scream at them. Tell them what stupid little idiots they were by creating so much noise and contaminating the evidence. But unless he wanted his paws cut to pieces, he had no option but to work his way cautiously towards them, hoping like hell he would not leave any blood on this floor. If he did, then the police would assume he was a suspect and although he'd wanted to go it alone in this house, he'd planned on being careful.

When he finally managed to pad his way through the mess, he arrived at the door, barged through into a corridor, and knocked them all rudely aside. "You bunch of blundering idiots," he snarled, "Are you frigging insane? Look at me. How am I supposed to detect and inspect when I'm covered with the stench of fags and booze?"

As the four small dogs stood in a line against the corridor wall, their tails now hanging limply behind them, he marched back and forth hissing and spitting like an angry Sergeant Major. Now oblivious to his surroundings, and still smarting from the embarrassment of falling into a pile of rubbish, he barked out orders and reprimands. "When I say don't go into the house, I mean don't go into the house," he snapped, "We're on a mission here... this is not some stupid game... lives are at risk... when we're on patrol and I give a command, you obey it! There is one leader here and that leader is me," he yelled, as his army ego reached epic proportions, "Do you lot understand?" He glared down at them. "If you don't understand then you can either bog off now or stand and fight!"

It took him five minutes to calm down. By the time he had finished, the four dogs were seated, tails held to attention, ears flat to their heads. He gritted his teeth and turned away. When silence finally descended, Zulu plucked up the courage to speak. "Sir," he coughed, "Erm, we're like really sorry." He looked to the others for support, but none was forthcoming, which George felt was typical of this little lot. Zulu had more courage than the lot of them put together he thought, or more determination he supposed, given the circumstances.

He told them all that their apologies were useless unless they changed their behaviour and respected his army dog experiences. "Whilst we're in this house," he snapped, "I want you all behind me. I shall sniff and look around the house first, you lot come behind me and see if I miss anything. We go slowly, quietly and we do not shake our fur all over the place, leave muddy paw prints or go to the toilet and we talk in whispers, okay."

The four small dogs affirmed their agreement with the plan. With that done, George recovered his senses enough to realise that the corridor they stood in, by the kitchen door, was similar to his own at home. The corridor led in two directions. One towards his left, swinging at right angles towards the back door behind the kitchen, the other to his right, a mere two meters away, to another door, which luckily was open. He presumed the door would lead into the lounge. It was no doubt set up in a similar manner as his own.

He told the others to form a head to tail formation with Charlie then Zulu behind him, but they were not to enter until he gave the command to do so.

When George poked his head through the door, he found himself staring at a replica of his own lounge. The lounge was so tiny there was little room to make any radical changes with furniture arrangements. The sofa sat in front of the back window and the table stood in front of the front window, the same setting as his own. If it weren't for the powerful smell of death, the lingering stench of tobacco and the sheer ugly, mess of the place, he would have assumed he was home.

The place looked like a bomb had hit it. Dirty plates and cups, more shredded newspapers and mail covered every surface. Layers of rumpled up blankets and torn old cushions covered the sofa. More ash trays lay around the sofa, overflowing toxic butts onto the bare threaded carpet. Shabby old books stood in odd piles against the walls along with magazines and old video cassettes. Numerous picture frames with photos covered the walls. They were all pictures of a cat, who he presumed was Elizabeth.

A large metal box shaped object with a glass screen stood to one side of the sofa and George assumed this was the TV. The old woman was not only twenty years behind the times in modern technology, she had also not bothered to clean up in twenty years. Cat hairs lay everywhere. He could feel them brushing up in between his paws. The place was disgusting. It would take the police months to find any relevant DNA in amongst this lot and it'd take him ages to find any clues too.

He stepped further into the lounge and noticed at once what Zulu had seen. In front of the sofa, was a carefully painted white outline of what he presumed had been the old bat's body. The body had laid in a cross shape with legs straight out in front and arms outstretched from her shoulders. There was a large but faded brownish stain on the carpet by her neck and chest and George could smell it was blood. He could not smell dog breath though or see any visible signs that a dog had been present. He skirted around the tiny white painted outline and again found nothing of note. His frustration grew. He had expected the sniff of dog saliva in amongst that blood or at least around the body but there was nothing. No paw prints, no dog hairs, no nothing.

He told the others to wait in the doorway until he had finished sniffing around the lounge. He was determined to find that dog, or the gun, so he sniffed and searched every inch of the carpet. This was difficult as multiple boot prints now covered the carpet, which he assumed belonged to the police. He cursed the cops for their incompetence. They could have easily trodden on a paw print and now he was at his wits end trying to find one.

However, as he neared the table, he sniffed something underneath it. As he moved in closer, he realised it was a paw print. A bloodied paw print, under the table and barely visible but a paw print, nevertheless. Not only that, but he could smell the distinct odour of dog urine. With these two clues, George knew he had discovered the culprit. The very dog who had been present and presumably half-eaten the old bat's neck.

Chapter 15

0330 hours

George slunk under the table slowly. Even from this distance he could see it was a large paw print. It was not bigger than his, but it was definitely not smaller. This at least meant that the dogs in the corridor were innocent. He moved towards the small dot of urine left by the dog. When he did, he was surprised. The sheer force of fear that emitted from that urine was so strong that George was surprised he had not found a much larger puddle of urine and a pile of dog poo as well. This dog had been terrified. Yet careful too.

He sniffed again, discovered it was a male dog, and then realised he had smelt a similar smell that very night. In amongst that tiny dot of urine was the very same concoction of emotions that he had sniffed in Zulu's urine: Despair, anger, and hopelessness. Yet, unlike Zulu's urine, there was a level of aggression and madness that he had only ever smelt from the dogs at war. He knew at once that this dog had been forced to help commit a murder and had gained no pleasure from it. Clearly, the dog had done his duty and then hidden under the table, an act which George knew only too well, for it was only in terror that he himself hid under the table. He found himself pitying the dog for it was clearly unhappy about the murder. However, without big police boot prints stamping on the evidence, this dog, if found, would have been accused of murder and then executed.

George tried to ascertain the dog's breed. This was difficult as the emotions of the dog took precedence over any other piece of information, but gradually, with some persistence, he was able to detect the faint odour of Doberman. A mad, terrified, angry Doberman who was no doubt completely and utterly loyal to his human, for despite his fear, he had only left the tiniest clue to his presence.

He trotted sadly over to the other dogs who were all peering through the doorway, eyes wide with fear.

"Well," he sighed, "I've found our murdering mongrel, but it's not good. I know the breed, sex and size of the dog but I can't detect any other human apart from the police."

"What do you mean it's not good," hissed Zulu. "If you've found that murdering mongrel dog who set up my human then that's got to be good surely?"

George sighed again. He knew Zulu was out for blood and he had no doubt that if he found the dog, he'd try to rip it to shreds, even if he would be at a distinct disadvantage being so small.

"Zulu," he said, "This dog is big and dangerous. But now I've got the sniff of him, I think he is also a victim. I don't think he wanted to help kill the old bag. I think he was forced to do it and I don't think he liked it at all."

"What are you saying," said Charlie. "That this dog was obeying the orders of someone more powerful than he?"

"Absolutely, Charlie. This dog, a Doberman no less, was terrified. If you don't believe me then check out the smell of his dog pee under the table."

Charlie strutted over to the table, followed swiftly by Zulu, Sid and Rocky. As the four dogs examined the evidence, George decided to go over the crime scene again. He was sure there must be another clue. It seemed as if the police had done nothing except remove the body. No doubt they figured that as they had their culprit, Zulu's human, they had no need to consider other alternatives.

He started with the sofa. He assumed that the old bat had been lying on it when she was accosted and murdered. She was probably lying there half cut on booze when the human culprit had dragged her to the floor, shot her and got the dog to rip out her throat. It would have been an easy murder with one so drunk. In fact, she may have already been laying on the floor when the murderer arrived.

He'd seen his own human in a similar state when she had drunk her bottle of vodka. Despite her efforts to get off the sofa and to her bed, sometimes she'd only made it as far as the lounge floor and had then spent the whole night snoring like a freight train. He recalled feeling damn annoyed about it. Without her faculties intact it meant that he had to sacrifice his sleep in a bid to stand guard over her in case of intruders or in case she died from alcohol poisoning. He briefly wondered if with age, his crazy human would turn out like the old bat, surrounded by hundreds of vodka bottles and endless photos of himself standing proudly next to a black beard. The thought turned his stomach and he vowed he would do his utmost to ensure she found happiness, outside of her bottle of vodka and regardless of the post-traumatic stress disorder she was clearly suffering from.

At once he got back to the business of sniffing the sofa. If there had been a struggle between the killer and the old bat, then he was sure it would have been on this sofa. He did not have to detect for long. As he rummaged around with his nose, he found to his horror that he was face to face with his enemy, again! With a warning growl interspersed with a nervous vocal tremor, he found himself backing away from the sofa. He couldn't believe it. He could see it. Right there. Sticking out from behind a cushion as clear as daylight, mocking him with its presence like some kind of reoccurring nightmare.

Upon hearing his growl, the other dogs flocked around him and stared in unison at the cushion he was glaring at.

"Hey," said Zulu suddenly, "That's a piece of my human's black beard. How did that get there?" He trotted over to the sofa and sniffed around the cushion. "It is my human's beard. It's a piece that he cut off before the murder. What's it doing behind this cushion?"

"Only a piece you say?" asked George as he paced carefully towards the beard. A piece he could deal with. A whole beard he could not. When he sniffed it, he almost vomited on the floor. "For Dogs' God, Zulu! Did your human actually drink that rum or did he just pour it over his beard. This thing reeks of alcohol."

"But how did it get there?" said Zulu as he pushed the cushion aside to reveal a clump of beard. "Look. It's a bit of the beard he cut off. A huge clump. This makes it look like my human was here, like he did it and he was the murderer."

"Well maybe he was," snarled Sid. "Maybe he did do the job, but no one thought he'd be accused because he's a cop so that's why they needed to lie, to ensure he got caught."

"That's rubbish, Sid," snarled Zulu with a venom he'd not used before. "It's obvious what's happened here. The murderer has grabbed a clump of beard from the street and placed it here to make it look like my human was guilty."

"Yeah, right," sneered Sid, "Like the murderer had been sitting out in the street all night waiting for your human to cut off his beard. How convenient for the murderer. This looks more like the old bat pulled out a clump of your human's beard in the struggle."

"But what about the Doberman, Sid?" asked Charlie. "Why and how could Zulu's human suddenly have access to the services of a Doberman in the middle of the night? It's not Zulu who's been here. It's not his paw print."

"Well maybe he nipped to the cop-shop and got a police dog," said Sid. "I'm sure he'd know Zulu well enough to know he wouldn't have the guts to be involved in a murder."

George gritted his teeth. Ever since the fight outside, Sid had been sucking up to Zulu and eating humble pie. Now the shaggy little hound was out to get him again. "Enough," he snarled, "Enough of this nonsense, Sid. The clump of beard is obviously evidence, but so is the fake black beard that smelt like the postie, the large paw print and smell of the Doberman under the table. Zulu's right. It looks like a set up. However, Sid has a point, and it can't be ignored. Until we find this Doberman and his murdering human, we have no choice but to go on with the hunt. I think we've done enough here. We should go outside and follow the trail of Elizabeth. The postie stole the cat, he's implicated in drug running, even if he is a red herring," he said, glaring at Charlie, "and he also started the rumours and death threats. Plus, he conveniently found the old bat dead this morning. It would have been too easy for him to have planted a bit of beard as evidence against Zulu's human. I say we go now and follow those boot prints out by the fence-line."

"I agree," said Charlie, "But first I think we should explore the rest of the house. We might find drugs, we might find the gun, or we might find nothing. But as we're here, we should at least look."

George agreed. They hunted and sniffed in every room, every corner and in every crevasse of that mouldy, damp house but all they found were more ashtrays, more empty bottles of booze and more dirt and clutter. They found no evidence of drugs, which made the reason Elizabeth was stolen or killed in the first place even more puzzling.

It was time to go but this time the four dogs slunk out of the cat flap quietly leaving George to work out how to get himself back onto the kitchen sideboard and through the window again.

Chapter 16

0400 hours

Following the boot prints along the side of the fence was easy. The prints were set in mud, and apart from the usual drizzle, it hadn't rained for days. There was only one problem. The old bat lived on the corner of the street, her house being the last one in a row. The boot prints simply tramped a trail for a few metres and then ended at a road. This meant that Elizabeth could have been loaded into a waiting vehicle and driven off somewhere. However, across the road lay another woody parkland, which also had houses and fences backing onto it. When Zulu, in his enthusiasm had raced across the empty road, he discovered that the boot prints continued along the fence-line, so, on the dogs trotted, once again in a head to tail formation with George now taking the lead.

As they slunk past the fences, a cacophony of dog barks and cat hisses assaulted their ears. They were in new territory now and the animals behind the fence lines knew it. When Charlie trotted up beside George, he felt a sense of comfort. He was fairly convinced of her innocence now and her part in this investigative role stood testament to that fact. He just hoped that the boot prints would lead them to the postie, for if the trail went cold, then he'd have nothing else to go on and Zulu's human would be left to rot in a cell.

They continued until they came to another road. The long line of houses they'd been trotting past suddenly stopped. There were no more fence lines to follow. George had felt sure they would have found the postie's house in amongst one of them.

Across the road stood a creepy looking church surrounded by grim looking gravestones and a small wooden fence with a rusty old gate. The gate swung open in the breeze and as it did so, it gave a slow menacing screech. On each side of the cemetery perimeter were a few bushes and trees and after that, the local pub, post office and grocery store. Not a human or animal could be seen along that road and darkness shrouded every building. Apart from the screeching gate and the odd toot from the local owl, all was silent.

The dogs were clearly nervous. None of them had ventured this far and the prospect of going any further, especially if it involved walking through that cemetery, was not appealing, even for George. However, George knew they could not stop now. If the postie wanted to keep a low profile whilst on a murder mission, the trees and bushes gave him plenty of coverage.

He pushed himself forwards towards the screeching gate and the creepy looking church. The others followed but at a more sedate pace. George decided to try the cemetery first. Maybe the postie had buried Elizabeth there. He pushed through the gate leaving it screaming hysterically behind him as it swung back and forth in a frenzied manner. This did nothing to add to the confidence of the four dogs behind him and he sniggered quietly as he heard a few frantic protests from the back of the line.

As George slunk cautiously towards the church along the gravel pathway, he heard a low, menacing growl behind him. When he backtracked, he found Zulu hunched over a boot print. The boot print was the exact size and shape of the posties, and it tramped another trail through and in between the gravestones. George congratulated Zulu on his find, and they set off again, following a windy trail past the gravestones and over the bodies beneath.

George lost count of the number of graves they walked over. It seemed the boot prints had no concern or respect for the dead. A cold shiver crept down his spine as he tried to imagine the type of person that belonged to these prints.

Finally, they came to another gate, except this one remained staunchly closed. Luckily, George had been trained in the art of opening doors, gates, and windows and for him, this gate was easy. As the gate swung open, it gave off such a vicious howl that George was tempted to rip the damn thing to shreds.

The gates were acting as if some heinous crime had been committed, as if he and the other dogs were guilty of something. He trotted on, keen to get away from this supposed human sanctuary.

As George and the others followed the trail, they found they were gradually entering a woodland that became darker and denser as they progressed. The boot prints stomped on determinedly though, clearly oblivious to the deepening darkness and the twisted trees, which loomed up above them. The moon was barely visible now, but the dogs ploughed on, despite the heightened beat of their thudding hearts.

Finally, they entered a clearing. It really wasn't that far away from the church, but they had walked at such a slow pace, it now seemed as if they were in the middle of nowhere, far from the safety of the cosy little village. The moon was back again and shone down with full force upon an old stone bridge. Beneath the bridge was a river. It was as dark as ebony and wove a slow silky path towards a small lake. The boot prints went neither left nor right, so it was clear they had made their way over the bridge.

George set off at once, not wishing to waste any time. However, as he neared the middle of the bridge, he realised the four dogs had not followed him. He turned to look and saw Charlie standing slightly in front of the little pack whilst the others hunched round her. It looked like they were supporting her for she had a look of pure terror in her eyes, a look she tried to hide, but it was not lost on George. "What's the go, Charlie," he hissed, "Are you coming or what?"

Charlie flattened her ears and turned away. Her ever-confident tail drooped listlessly behind her and as she glanced again at George, he saw that haunted look, the same one he'd seen at the den when she'd challenged him to question her past. There was a long pause as the others waited for her response.

Then suddenly, as if the incident had never occurred, Charlie tightened her jaw and began marching towards him. Her brandy eyes turned as cold as frost as they glared out from beneath her balaclava. She raised her jaw and stared straight at him. George was no fool. He knew that look. It meant do not ask any questions if you value your life, so he turned and trotted on, wondering sadly why Charlie was scared of a bridge.

The boot prints turned sharply to the left of the bridge and followed a trail along the river until the river branched out and formed a lake. George thought the lake quite beautiful. The ebony water was as shiny and still as a new penny. In the middle of the lake, about twenty metres away, stood a large white statue. The statue was moulded into the shape of three male soldiers, one kneeling and two standing, all three with guns aimed at some non-existent enemy.

162

George noticed the absence of a war dog, and this saddened him. There should have been a war dog there, he thought as he turned sharply to the right again and followed the boot prints away from the lake. Dogs did the most dangerous job of all in a war and yet this statue seemed to ignore that fact. It reminded him of Sadie and of all his war dog friends who had either died in combat or been put down, once they'd past their use by date.

He tramped on, trying to ignore the bitter twist of fury in his heart. He wondered what Charlie was thinking as she marched behind him. He could well imagine her reaction to the statue, and this made him smile. She would not hold back on her anger nor mince her words. Unlike most beings, she spoke her truth without regard for the consequences, but she ensured her fortress remained thick and strong. He admired that and he admired her. She was still irritatingly arrogant, but he now knew that was just her way of protecting herself.

As he paced ever onwards, he decided he had grown quite fond of her and so it was with some horror that he suddenly felt a sharp pain shoot up his tail. As he turned to look, he saw it was Charlie who now had his tail clamped tightly in between her buttery jaws. The look in her eyes said, 'don't move and don't bark or I'll chomp down harder'.

This sudden movement of aggression was a shock. He nearly threw her across the ground until he realised why she had stopped him in his tracks. Right before him, beyond the bushes, stood a metal fence-line and within that, sat a small stone farmhouse beside a large wooden shed. As his eyes zoomed in on the boot prints before him, he saw them tramp a trail through the bushes, towards the fence and then onwards through a metal gate and towards the tiny farmhouse. If Charlie hadn't stopped him, he would have trotted straight into the den of the enemy.

163

They had found the postie's warren, but it was a disheartening site. George had hoped the postie would at least have some neighbours who they could run to for support. But this house and that shed, stood alone, nestled in amongst the trees, cold, dark, and silent.

Chapter 17

0430 hours

The five dogs hunkered down behind the bushes to watch and wait.

If anyone were in the house, they were clearly asleep or out for the night. The lights were off, the TV was off and there was nothing to indicate the presence of humans. A red postal van sat alongside another car in the driveway. The car looked black, shiny, and new. Compared to the shabby old cars in the village of Titchfield, this car had clearly cost a lot more money. The dogs remained silent, watching, listening, sniffing.

"I smell Elizabeth," said Zulu suddenly, and without neither a whisper nor a nervous tremor.

"Shhh," hissed Charlie, "Keep your voice down, Zulu."

"Sorry," he replied, now in a whisper, "but can you smell her? Can you smell Elizabeth?"

"I can certainly sniff the scent of cat," Charlie hissed, "but I'll wager there's more than one cat in there and more than one human."

"I agree," whispered George. "In fact, the smell of cat is overwhelming. It makes me want to vomit. If Elizabeth is alive, then I'll bet my right paw that she's in that house."

"Or in that shed," said Rocky, whose mammoth ears were now rotating on his tiny head like a pair of giant spotlights. The other dogs turned their ears towards the shed. As they concentrated their efforts, they heard the distinct sound of mewing. As George homed in towards the sound, he heard a high pitched, vicious yowl, which he quickly interpreted as, "Get lost you fat lazy Porker." This was swiftly followed by a deep, masculine yowl which said, "I wouldn't touch you with a friggin' bargepole, you ugly old bitch."

When George glanced at Zulu, he saw the grinning flash of white teeth. "It is her, Sir," he whispered, as his tail began to thrash back and forth in a frenzy. "It's Elizabeth and she's alive. I can't believe it. I'd not mistake that vindictive, nasty yowling if I tried."

"And nor can that male cat she's arguing with," said Sid, "She's obviously as popular amongst cats as she is dogs, not."

Before George could make any further plans or comments, a loud growl seemed to erupt from the earth before them. As their ears homed in towards the farmhouse, they heard another growl followed by a series of deep vicious barks. Before George could register the fact that the wind had turned and was now blowing in behind them, toward the tiny farmhouse, he saw a sudden streak of black race at a maddening pace towards him. As the moon shone down upon the racing form, he saw a frightening set of gleaming white fangs, and as the dog drew up to the gate, he saw the coal black eyes of madness glaring through the bushes and straight into his soul.

"Don't move, anyone," said George through gritted teeth as the big black dog stood squarely at the gate and barked aggressively in their direction. In the bushy silence around them, the barks were deafening. The five dogs were as still as statues and George thanked Dogs' God that they had the good sense not to move. That fence was tall, but still short enough for the dog to jump if necessary. George didn't want to give the dog an excuse to jump and chase his newfound prey. He lowered his eyes and stared at the ground and with a sidelong glance, he saw the other four dogs had done the same. Eye contact with this vicious fiend would be suicide. But running off was not an option either.

As the dog barked on relentlessly, he figured that this must be the murdering Doberman they'd sniffed in the old bat's lounge. The dog had been mad, he recalled, but terrified too. He had no doubt that this was the very same dog. He'd seen the madness in the dogs' eyes. For sure, the dog had every right to be angry and defend his territory, but the sheer anger that emitted from this dog was not normal as far as he was concerned. From the corner of his eye, he could see the saliva dripping from the dog's jaws. If the dog jumped the fence, they'd all be dead.

But before he could contemplate why a crazy dog, who clearly knew there were five dogs hiding out behind the bushes, did not jump the fence, a light flicked on in the house. Suddenly, a man appeared in the doorway. It was the postman. There was no mistaking him. George could smell the creeping, conniving sweat of the man.

The postman began jumping up and down, waving his fist furiously and yelling at the barking dog, but the dog barked on regardless. George noted that the postie was stick thin, which looked at odds with his stripy pyjamas that flapped around him. As the dog barked louder, the postie began screaming, his face now red with fury as his thin white hair and bushy white beard glimmered in the moonlight.

The posties efforts were fruitless. The Doberman was adamant that there was something to bark about and clearly the postman had no authority over this dog.

Then another man appeared on the porch. It was then that George felt Charlie stiffen. She was lying beside him, her heart hammering away in tune with his, and appropriately so, given the circumstances. However, when the second man arrived, he heard her heart increase into a frantic gallop, and it soon became clear why.

This man, in comparison to the postie, was a monster. George could smell it. The anger and hatred that emitted from this man's sweat swept towards him like a tidal wave. He had never, in his whole entire army career smelt anything as threatening and horrific from a human, even from this distance. As his eyes zoomed in towards the man, he saw that he was built like a barrel, his chest protruding from his legs like a war tank ready to roll over anyone in its way. His thighs were chunky, and his shaven head stood on his shoulders like a rocky boulder, without need for a neck, for his neck was as thick as his head.

Unlike the postie, this man was dressed in black jeans with a short, black, woolly jumper. It was as if he were ready for combat at any given moment. Ready to kill, maim or torture anyone in his way. George could see the man's eyes as the light from the doorway bounced off him. They were dark and as hard as steel. There was nothing in them that reminded him of any human he'd ever met. Even in the war he had seen fear, compassion, and love. Even from the enemy. This man had nothing inside his soul. He was pure evil, and George knew at once why Charlie had stiffened. She saw it too.

The man did a quick visual scan of the farmyard and then stared out at the woods around them. At one point, he seemed to stare straight in their direction, but each dog quickly lowered their gaze.

The man saw nothing though, for despite his size, he was not equipped to either see, smell, or hear the five dogs crouching in the bushes. When he spoke, it was in a deep, gruff voice with a tone so hard it made Charlie's cold, clipped tones seem like honey. "It's probably another damn rabbit. Bloody stupid dog."

He then began yelling at the Doberman, ordering him to "shut the hell up," but the dog, despite the evil behind him, barked on. The dog was trained to protect his master no matter what and five dogs unescorted by humans would have been classified as danger. As his barking grew in intensity and threatened to burst the eardrums of everyone concerned, the two men remained oblivious to the dog's frantic efforts to alert them. Instead, they were angry and seemed to blame the dog for his barking.

Then the monstrous man started marching towards the Doberman. He was still yelling at the dog to shut it, but the dog barked on, his bark getting ever more frenzied and vicious. So engrossed in his duty as guard dog and in a blind rage, which was more than a match for the fury the man exhibited, the Doberman was oblivious to the encroaching danger that strode towards him from behind. The man held in his hand a large piece of wood. It was as thick as his arm, and it was clear he intended to use it on the dog.

Despite this, the dog, ever faithful to its master, barked on until suddenly there was a piercing yelp as the man whacked him over the back with the wood. He whacked again and the dog lay down on his stomach and whined. George gritted his teeth. He felt like he was being attacked as well. It took all his energy not to race out and rescue that dog.

"You stupid dumb dog," yelled the monster. "Do you wanna' alert the whole village to our whereabouts!" and with that he grabbed the dog's collar and dragged him towards the house. "You're gonna get the friggin' hose for this, you idiot dog. Why are you always barking for no good reason? When I tell you to shut it, I mean shut it!"

As the monster dragged the now quivering dog along the pathway, the dog seemed to finally give up. Instead of straining against the man, he now trotted beside him as if consigned to his fate. The monster yelled at the postie, "Grab the hose will yer'? A good dousing of freezing water should quieten him up for the night!"

The five dogs watched in horror as the man led the Doberman around to the back of the house. As the postie slammed the front door and went inside, George heard a low, ominous growl from Charlie.

Suddenly she stood up on her short stout legs which were now trembling. As her growl increased in volume, George recognised immediately what was happening. Charlie was about to hurl herself forward, straight into the den of the enemy. The rage and fear which emitted from her fur was the very same he himself had begun to experience in the war. That same hatred that had led to his loss of control and that maddening desire to tear apart the enemy.

Before she had time to launch herself out from among the bushes, he grabbed her in his jaws by the scruff of her neck. As she twisted about helplessly, snarling like a psychotic maniac, he turned and raced off with her, back down the pathway towards the lake.

Running along holding a thrashing ball of fur in his jaws was no easy task. When he finally made it to the lake, where the three male statues remained standing with rifles at the ready, he managed with one last burst of energy to hurl Charlie as far as he could, straight into the depths of the icy black lake.

As George sat by the water's edge, Sid, Rocky and Zulu arrived, panting with exertion and the shock at this unexpected turn of events. As their beating hearts began to still, they stared intensely at the water. Charlie had not yet emerged.

Chapter 18

0500 hours

Time seemed to stop for the four dogs as they waited patiently for Charlie to bob to the surface and then swim towards them. In fact, it was only about ten seconds, but ten seconds under water was far too long. In that time George had stopped breathing. He had wanted to shock her back to her senses, not drown her. But she'd not appeared. Was she dead? She had made a fairly large splash when she entered the water, but now already, the lake had begun to still again.

When her head suddenly bobbed up from the surface, the four dogs let out a huge sigh of relief. But this was short lived. Instead of swimming gracefully towards them as all dogs should, because all dogs can swim, Charlie started flailing about helplessly in the same spot. She seemed oblivious to their presence or their encouraging barks as they tried in vain to guide her back to the shore. Instead, she seemed to swim in circles, bobbing under water

173

every few seconds, only to emerge choking and coughing as the water splashed around her.

Sid turned to glare at George. "You stupid idiot," he growled, "She's scared of water. She obviously can't swim."

Before George could consider this, Zulu leapt into the lake and swam towards Charlie. As he circled in behind her with a speed and skill that would match any otter or fish, George was reminded of a nuclear submarine. He watched in awe as Zulu grabbed Charlie by the scruff of her neck and swam back, paddling sideways as he tried to keep her thrashing body afloat. When he finally got near the shore, Sid and Rocky decided to help haul her in.

George sat there transfixed by the scene as the three little dogs tried to lick her now still body back to life.

It was only when Zulu paused to yell at George, "Bloody well get here and help," that he moved from his spot and with a tongue five times the size of the others, he licked in a frenzy, feeling the panic start to rise from his throat.

It took a full minute to revive Charlie. When finally, she rolled over and vomited out a belly full of water, the four dogs ceased their licks and then flocked in around her to warm her icy body with their thick, dry, fur. They lay there for five minutes until the violent shivers, which to George felt like major convulsions, slowed to a halt.

When the four dogs backed off to give her space, George felt his heart contract. Gone was her staunch, macho, arrogant image. Instead, her waterlogged fur seemed to have shrunk her to half of her original size. As she slowly sat up, her eyes remained fixed on the muddy ground and her great pyramid ears flopped down beside her golden jaws and soggy face mask. The proud and gritty fighter in her had left and instead, George noted, sat a scared little dog who bowed her head in shame.

George felt his stomach do a double flip. This was not what he'd expected. Not part of his plan. He'd just wanted to cease the tide of rage that was threatening to overtake her. If she had raced towards the fence like a maniac, she would have put both her life and those of the others at risk. Although he'd seen many dogs suffer great pain and trauma in the war, he had never in a thousand years ever expected to see such a strong little dog pose such a pathetic little figure. He glanced at the other three dogs and noticed them glaring at him. Their eyes seemed to say, "So, is that what you planned for our beloved leader? Is this how you war dogs treat your own?"

He was speechless of course. No matter how Charlie behaved, she always seemed to render him mute. He had wanted desperately at one point, to gain some smug satisfaction at seeing her defensive walls crash down around her, but now they had, he felt awful. But trotting back to his comfy sofa, although appealing, was not an option. It was he who had to bring her back to life for it was he who had nearly, albeit unwittingly, nearly ended it.

George shifted uncomfortably on his rump, raised his tail, and wagged it in an apologetic manner. He coughed out his apology to Charlie and the others and then tried to explain, although at that moment, his reasoning, although logical, did not stop the tide of anger that swept his way from Charlie's supporters.

"Well, again, I am sorry, Charlie. I didn't realise you couldn't swim. I mean, well, most dogs can swim, and I thought that such a strong little dog like you, so skilled at survival an' all, well I thought that swimming would be nothing to you."

George's plan to start working on her ego seemed to do the trick as finally Charlie appeared to rally herself and gather some strength.

At last, she raised her head and stared directly at him. When she spoke, the clipped tones were back. "Inspector, as furious as I am that you damn well nearly killed me, I've enough sense to know that was not your intention. Furthermore, it is not your fault." She turned and glared into the night, straight in the direction of the farm. Without turning back to him she said, "That monstrosity back there, that disgusting example of a human being, was my original human. My master." Her voice seemed to fade out then, and when she spoke again, it was in quiet monotones.

She told the pack that she had been one of five siblings born to a foxy mother who had delivered her eighth litter. "My mother was beautiful. She would have done anything to protect us, but when it came to our master, she was powerless. Her time with him had ensured she had become sick in body and mind. The horrors she had experienced under his rule, the puppies she had seen killed or taken away meant that she'd lost her spirit. But she still had love for us, Inspector. That never left her, right up until the very end."

As the other dogs sat in awe of this tiny dog, she told them the story of her life under this cruel dictator. "When my mother served no purpose to him, he shoved her in a sack. She had kept the five of us puppies warm and she had given as much advice to us as she could. But to me, her passive stance towards this man was wrong and it was not until I lived the full measure under his rule that I began to see how she'd lost her fighting spirit. "Be nice," she always said, "Just obey, for there is nothing more out there in the world." And for my mother that meant that her last few breaths were spent gasping for breath underwater, in a sack filled with stones."

She told them that she had lived somewhere different then. It was more of a town than a village and the river was more like a dirty canal. But, she explained, they still lived on an isolated patch of land, so the monster could manufacture his drugs on the quiet. "And the people who visited were as dependant on him as we were. They got drugs, they earned money and they were cruel."

176

She spoke of the beatings that Blow and herself received, but most of all, she spoke of the torture they suffered with his chosen method – water. "He would try and drown me and Blow in a bucket of water," she continued, as her slow, monotones sent the four dogs into a hypnotic trance. "Or he'd put the freezing cold hose on us. Either way, I developed a fear of water. The only way myself and Blow survived those attempted drownings were to play dead. If we purposely made our body's go limp, then he'd release us, and laugh."

She then went on to explain again how Blow had desperately tried to follow his mother's advice and please them. He had taken their drugs, but he'd become a paranoid, nervous wreck, and the joke of all the master's friends. "He died on world cup night," said Charlie, and as she told them the story of her brother's death, and how he was forced to do his drowning act, her demeanour changed. No longer was she a drenched and pathetic mess.

George saw a distinct change. The wall she had clearly constructed to protect herself from all this began to rebuild itself. A wall that had helped her to survive physically and mentally, but had meant sacrificing her softer, kinder, more vulnerable side. A side where trust could not possibly exist, nor a sense of powerlessness, for to her, that simply meant death.

"When I realised the drowning was going on for too long, it was too late. I raced up to my master and bit him on the wrist. But when he released my beautiful brother, I realised he was dead."

Charlie went on to explain how she had tried to revive him to no avail. She then had dragged him in to the laundry where they slept, still licking him frantically as her panic mounted. The other dogs sank down on their paws in horror. If dogs could weep like humans, they would have done so, for Charlie's tale and that of her brother was the saddest story of all.

177

Charlie, however, was angry. Her hard exterior had resurfaced and as she glared up at the cold, white moon, it seemed as if the hatred she emitted would shatter the moon into a thousand pieces.

"I took my brother with me when I left. Whilst the monster drank on into the night, I pulled Blow through the dog flap and dragged him for miles, as far away as possible. Far from humans, far from houses, away from the drugs and greed, which seem to dominate humanity. When I got to the woods, I buried my brother in a muddy hole. I stayed there for weeks, surviving on rats and mice, until they got my presence, and they moved on. So, in desperation, I had to leave the grave of my brother and I travelled, chasing rats and rabbits for food.

"I lived alone, for no other animal would befriend me and really, I don't blame them. I hated everyone then, even other animals because of their passive acceptance of human dominance. When I spoke to some of them about rising up and revolting, they always went vague and made some excuse to wander off. Every animal has been brainwashed into accepting that humans can do as they please. It was that knowledge that finally broke me. Not the lack of food, but the lack of fighting spirit in the animal kingdom." She turned and glared at George. "That's why I despise humanity, Inspector and that is why I teach my pack to fight!"

It was a sad moment for all the dogs. They had all suffered something in the hands of their greedy humans and it seemed as if there was no answer to it all. As if no matter what they did, the humans would always win. That ultimately the destruction of the animal species would see the demise of them all.

It was Zulu who managed to barrel his way into their pit of despair and rally them back into action. After all, he argued, humans were bad, but not all humans. Some were decent and kind and suffered their own misery at the hands of other humans.

"My human is not like your monster, Charlie. He would never commit such heinous crimes. He is a good man and no matter what you say about humans, I still stand by him."

Charlie shook the water off her fur. "You may be right, Zulu. There exists good and bad amongst us all. Although, knowing who to trust is a hard task. So, on that note, I vote we continue with our mission. It is clear to me now what has happened. My old master, though master is too good a word, has obviously abducted Elizabeth and since it was clearly him who did this, then I have no hesitation in believing that it was he who murdered the old bat. Though, as yet, we have no evidence, I say that we go on in and expose that bastard for the monster he is!"

Chapter 19

0545 hours

The four little dogs sat in silence as George finished telling them his plan. They were still by the lake after deciding it was safer to talk there than to return to the postie's farmhouse.

"I don't like it," growled Charlie, "The risk to Zulu is too high."

George stared down at the little black dog who stared back, his small chocolate eyes glimmering in the moonlight. However, he was no longer curled up in a defensive little ball, for indeed, since the night had begun, Zulu had changed. Gone was the naivety, the hopelessness, and the lack of confidence he'd previously exhibited. Instead, his ears stood tall and alert and although his hind legs still quivered, his eyes shone with courage and excitement.

The other two dogs pawed absently at the ground. Clearly, they too were unsure that Zulu could do the task.

"Regardless of what the others think, Zulu, do you think you're up to the job?" said George.

Zulu stood and wagged his tail enthusiastically. "Sir, I believe I can do it. If this is our best bet, then, yes."

Charlie gave another grunt of disapproval. She was clearly very unhappy with the plan. "Inspector, despite my desire to enact total and utter revenge on that monster out there, I do not want Zulu dying in the process. A fast runner he may be, but that Doberman is five times his size and could outrun him in an instant."

Zulu turned calmly to Charlie, as the tip of his tail wiggled in his ever-grateful manner. But instead of shrinking and cowering at her, he stood tall and proud. "Charlie, you have trained me well in the art of ducking and diving. The three of you chased me relentlessly night after night and in truth, there was never a single time that you actually caught me without my consent."

At this Charlie growled, her own pride taking over, but Zulu barrelled on. "Plus, I was able to fight three of you off, so I think my fighting skills are enough to get me out of any difficult situations. I am small, fit and supple and that Doberman, even if he caught me, would be unlikely to hold onto me for long."

"A second in the jaws of that deranged dog would be enough, Zulu," Charlie growled.

"Yes, but of all of us, I do have the longest and fastest legs. Apart from the Inspector, of course, but even then, my legs move at triple the speed of any big dog and I now know this terrain like the back of my paw. I very much doubt that Doberman gets out much and when he does, he's probably lagging along on a lead."

"Yes, maybe, Zulu. But surely our Inspector here would be better at the role he is giving you. He is bigger, can run fast, no doubt, after his time in the war and he can fight back. The odds of him overcoming this Doberman are much higher."

George disagreed. "I'm not disputing your logic, Charlie, but despite my size and fighting skills, that dog is still younger and fitter than me, so if it came to a fight, he could still win, or worse,

I could win but only by killing him. Besides, the noise would wake the whole neighbourhood. No. The idea here is not to cause harm or kill. It is more to distract him, get him over the fence and lead him away from the farm. My skills would be better served in other areas."

Charlie was still not happy. "How about I just stroll up to the fence and tell him my story then? If I say I had escaped and that there was a life away from that monster, then maybe he'll agree to work with us."

George very much doubted it. "He won't be up for any cosy little chats, Charlie. You know that. You saw the madness in his eyes. He's trained to kill. Vicious and unpredictable. We just can't take the risk."

"But what if we tempt him out and then all attack him and rip out his throat?" asserted Sid. "Surely that's the safest bet?"

George was surprised at Sid's sudden desire to protect the lad but before he could intervene, Charlie said, "No Sid. That dog has suffered enough abuse. It would be preferable if he lived to see another day with a kinder human then die by the jaws of other animals. I don't want the dog harmed."

"Then it's back to my plan, isn't it," said George. "We know the dog is probably terrified of water. We saw him get threatened with the hose. We saw his reaction. We also saw yours. If Zulu tempts the dog over the fence, runs to the lake, swims to the statue, and stands on the platform, then taunts him or talks to him, then we might stand a chance. I very much doubt that dog will enter the water."

"You said the dog was mad, Inspector," argued Charlie, "He might be mad enough to swim regardless of his fear."

"Then if he does, I'll just swim over to the other side and run like hell back home and through my dog-flap," said Zulu, still brimming with confidence and excessive good cheer.

George wagged his tail in agreement. He knew about army strategies and picking out the best candidate for the job. Zulu's skill lay in his ability to run and weave, and his ability to swim was outstanding. Furthermore, if Zulu had any chance of entering into a dialogue with this dog, it would be him and him only, who would manage to charm the hind legs off the Doberman. Charlie, of course, could probably do so too, but she was too intimidating and full of equal rage.

"Sir," said Zulu, "I'll do it. For the love of my human, I will, even if I die trying, for I know you will find that cat and free my human. You've already proven your skill and determination to help, despite your fear of black beards. You know my human is innocent and I am certain that your sense of justice will ultimately lead to his freedom. Besides, if you dogs have to fight those humans, then you will need a big dog to help, one who is used to fighting them. For that, our Inspector is the best dog for the job."

The other three dogs, including George, had to agree. George knew too that these brave little dogs, especially Zulu and Charlie, deserved and needed his help, and he knew too that now, despite everything, for their sake, if need be, then he would have no hesitation ripping out the throats of those men.

When George told Zulu this, he wagged his tail then trotted up to George and licked him on the nose. "Thank you, Sir. No matter what happens, I will never forget you. None of us shall."

George spluttered with embarrassment. "No need for sentiment right now, Lad." Although secretly he felt quite emotionally overcome at the lad's gentle kiss. Before he could feel that piercing pain through his heart, the same one he always felt when he thought of Sadie, he lifted his ears and tail and growled, "My friends, we must all wrap ourselves up in our most hardened exteriors now, for we face a terrible enemy. One who will stop at nothing, not even torture or murder.

"So, if we are to outsmart this fiend, then there must be no soft sentiments, no looking back, no changing our plan. We must go forth with all the bravery we can muster. And again, I must reiterate, in this instance, you must all follow my command. No impulsive acts of bravery," he growled, turning to Charlie, "Only when I give the word, do we move and when I say stop, we stop, okay?"

The others agreed and he saw them all stiffen, their tails held high and proud. Their pyramid ears rotated like satellites on their tiny heads, their jaws stiffened, and their bristles poked out like daggers. They were ready, he thought. A motley little crew, an irritating, challenging pack, but with their better parts nurtured, a brave and cunning troop. George turned back to the farm.

"My friends, we go at once – Zulu to lead the Doberman away, us to the side fence so we can dig a tunnel to that shed."

Chapter 20

0615 hours

Of course, the plot to lead the Doberman away from the farm very much depended on whether he had been tied up or locked in the house. If he had, which Charlie doubted as he was still on guard, then the hose would have at least subdued him. Using a freezing cold hose to control his rage was, she reasoned, the same strategy that George had used to justify controlling Charlie's rage when he'd thrown her into the lake. George simply grunted when she reminded him of this. Zulu, however, said that getting the hose for something the Doberman had been right about in the first place, might only make him angrier when a second attack on his territory ensued.

There was only one way to find out. Ultimately, they wanted the Doberman to jump the fence and follow Zulu to the lake. It was with great reluctance though that the four dogs left Zulu at the first set of bushes they had been hiding behind when they'd first met the Doberman. As they crept round to the fence line near to the shed, they found some more bushes to hide behind to watch and listen.

It was Zulu's theory that was right in the end. When the little lad crashed loudly through the bushes towards the front gate, he'd barely arrived when suddenly the others saw a streak of black hurl itself down the garden path towards Zulu.

There was no time for talk, no time for any prancing about and taunting the dog as Zulu had planned. The Doberman, furious at being punished for a crime he'd not committed, was clearly determined to get his enemy, and tear him to pieces. Without warning, without even a snarl or a warning bark, the black dog leapt over the fence within seconds of Zulu arriving there. The dog was quick. The others looked on in horror. They'd imagined a slower response. More barking. Perhaps a few arguments. This dog had clearly been lying in wait, watching, smelling, listening for its enemy, and planning an attack of its own.

As the great mad dog flew through the air, Zulu turned on his paws and ran. His response was so quick that the others barely had a chance to see him flee. All they saw was the flash of a ginger diamond as it streaked through the bushes. No sooner had Zulu departed than the Doberman descended on the very same bushes and set forth, hot in pursuit.

As soon as George and the others saw Zulu dash off, they focused their efforts and began to dig. George had instructed them to dig a tunnel under the fence, quietly, without discussion and without further thought about Zulu's plight.

Within ten minutes they were under the fence and slowly padding their way towards the shed. They slunk in low and steady, ensuring the wind kept behind them. None of them talked.

George sensed their terror. He strode on, taking the lead. As they sidled up against the shed wall, George noticed a door.

They stood outside and listened. They could hear some minor scuffles, a few snores, and the gentle rattle of metal. Other than that, there was nothing. The smell of cat piss was overwhelming though. It had assaulted their noses from the fence, but at 30 metres away it had been a mild whiff.

Closer, it reeked. Yet George noted that it was not the usual stench of arrogant cats, but more a smell of fear and misery. These cats, he thought, were prisoners. It was not their choice to be stuck in that shed and if Elizabeth was in there, he had no doubt that there were other cats who had been abducted as well.

With more sniffs, George could place about seven different breeds. But his sniffing had taken some effort. Dissecting and analysing the combination of cat, terror, horror, and hopelessness was too much, so he considered the possibility of more than seven cats.

They had to be cautious now. Cats and dogs were natural predators. As such, they had an instinctual distaste and distrust of each other. If his little pack strode into the shed together, without explanation, the cats were likely to start shrieking and meowing. They could attack as well. The noise would wake up the monster and the postie.

He looked at the latch. It was an old wooden door, and the latch was rusted metal. All he had to do was lift the latch with his paw.

He glanced at the other dogs. They were all seated, huddled up against the wall of the shed, cold, shivering and staring up at him in horror. He knew they could smell the cats in the shed, and he knew they were all scared.

"I'm going to have to go in first. Alone," he hissed, partly to keep his voice low and partly to ensure they obeyed him. "I'm going to sneak through that door, announce my presence and tell these cats that I come in peace with a rescue party. I'm going to instruct them to remain silent. You all got that?"

They nodded their heads furiously.

"If it goes wrong, then get ready to run. Otherwise, I'll come back to get you, okay?"

More head nods. More shivering.

Slowly, he lifted the latch. He opened the door and entered the shed.

Chapter 21

0630 hours

It was dark at first. The sun had yet to rise and there were no windows. His eyes instinctively adjusted to accommodate the dark and when visibility hit, he felt like he'd been stabbed with a knife.

The scene before him was horrific: Like an unkept, hideous form of prisoner of war camp. Spread before him were countless cages made of wood and wire. The cages were lined up against three walls. They sat in stacks, some three or four high. Within each one he sensed two or more cats.

The fourth wall was divided in half. Workbenches and various tools made up one half. The other was clearly a garage door. Tables and workbenches were scattered down the middle of the shed. Perched atop these were yet more cages as well as bags of dried cat food and cat litter. The place stunk of cat piss, cat poo and cat vomit. Shredded newspaper and dry straw covered the shed floor.

Quickly, he counted the cages. By his calculations there was possibly a hundred if not more. If that were the case, then his initial estimate of seven cats was ridiculously miscalculated.

His stomach did a double flip. The urge to vomit was overpowering. Not just because of the stench, but also the shock. Never in his entire army career had he witnessed such a barbaric scene. He had seen blood, bones, fire, and death, which included his dog comrades, but this scene, this horror, was completely alien to him.

The captivity of humans he could handle. But the captivity of animals? Kept in such abhorrent conditions?

Visions of his warm, comfy sofa and bowlfuls of roast dinners emerged in his mind. Suddenly he felt guilty. Ungrateful. Whilst he had been snoozing away in despair, these poor little animals had been suffering mercilessly. All this time he had been worried about terrorists and bombs, yet all this time the enemy, the monstrosity on his doorstep, had been a sadistic drug baron and a skinny, pale postman.

This was a different type of war, he thought. One in which animals were kept captive and tortured, yet they had no voice to make their objections known to other humans. Animals who were living in hell but had no one to fight this war for them.

He felt a rage inside him begin to emerge. Quickly, he reigned it in. The smell of rage from a dog would scare these cats even more.

Suddenly he heard the cages begin to rattle around him. As he stared at them, he saw a hundred pair of yellow eyes glistening and gleaming straight in his direction.

Chapter 22

0645 hours.

"Shhhhh…" he whispered, but harshly enough for them to understand his urgency and loud enough for them to all hear. "I come in peace so do not be scared." He spoke quickly, before they all started meowing in fear. "My name is Inspector George Penkins and myself and my pack have come here tonight to rescue you all."

He sat down, flattened his ears, and lowered his tail. He knew they could see him. Cats were better at seeing in the dark than dogs.

"All of you," he continued, "Stay silent. The postie and the monster are asleep in the house. One of our pack has distracted the Doberman so we should be safe for now. Can one of you take leadership here and tell me if there is anything else we need to fear?"

Many of the cats hissed at him. Viciously enough to wake up yet more cats who glared through their bars suspiciously.

Quickly, he repeated his peace and rescue mission message, and requested one cat to converse with.

Suddenly, he heard a piercing screech. It came from the cage directly across from him. Inside, sat a small, slender feline with huge pyramid ears that perched atop her skinny face. She was hunched over, trying to squeeze herself between a huge fluffy ginger male and the wire mesh walls of their cage. Both glared at him intensely.

Immediately, he recognised her. Not just from her photos on the wall of the old bat's house, but from the stench of cat hairs and cat piss in her garden. His heart sank.

It was Elizabeth and she looked in no mood to be friendly and accommodating to George's wishes.

"Don't screech," he hissed. "You're Elizabeth, aren't you? The Cat who lives with the old bat, erm, I mean old lady next door to Zulu's human."

Immediately, she screeched again and with such venom that he knew instantly why Zulu despised her so much.

However, he also suspected that as a cat so unpredictable and arrogant, he'd need to liaise with her first. Plus quieten her down. Zulu was right. Elizabeth clearly hated dogs.

"Listen, Elizabeth." He spoke in low but urgent tones. "We, myself and my pack, have been looking for you all night. We've been to your house, and we've discovered the drugged fish you ate. Zulu…"

Another screech.

George's heart sped up. If she didn't shut up, she would ruin the plan.

"Zulu informed us of your plight."

Another blood curdling screech.

"Just shut the hell up," he snapped. "Jeez. We're here to help you. Help you all," he glanced around at the other cats. "If we're going to get you all out of here, we need you to be quiet."

She paused then. He saw her flatten her ears slightly. He also saw a flicker of hope in her eyes. There was no way she could get out of that cage from the inside, but if he let her out, she'd have some hope of escape. Even if she had to run or fight, at least she would have a chance. George saw her calculate all that, as her yellow and orange eyes flickered intensely in his direction.

She is worse than Charlie, he thought. By Christ, she is worse than the enemy at war. Possibly even the monster himself.

Then she spoke, in snakelike whispers and hisses. He felt a shiver sneak up his spine.

"So, you," she spat, "You, a mere dog, escorted by my mortal enemy, Zulu, claim to be here to rescue me and all of us cats? I don't believe you."

The fat, ginger male beside her spoke then. "Exactly," he hissed, "Why would a bunch of dogs come and rescue a shed full of cats. It ain't logical, if you don't mind my saying. Why should we believe you?"

This cat spoke in deep, guttural tones. George recognised the voice. It was the male cat who had been arguing with Elizabeth earlier.

Clearly, these two cats, the most despicable of the lot he thought, were taking leadership. The others were terrified. Already they had been through hell and the prospect of being supposedly rescued by a pack of dogs probably did sound horrifying.

"Look," continued George, "believe me. I never expected I'd ever be in charge of rescuing a bunch of cats. But frankly, nor have I ever seen such a sad and horrific scene. I mean for Dogs' God. What the hell have these monsters got planned for you all? Are

195

you being sold as pets? Have you all been abducted like Elizabeth?"

One of the cats started sobbing quietly. A few more joined in. George shushed them again.

"They're terrified, obviously," said the male, in more amenable, albeit patronising, tones. "Although, if we were being sold as pets then we'd all welcome it. Unfortunately, for us, not so. Many of us are strays, picked up in the city. A few, like myself and Elizabeth here, are pedigrees. But that makes no difference. Not for our fate anyway."

"Which is?" George asked.

"The fur trade, Inspector," stated Elizabeth, "Today the lorry arrives, and we will all be taken to the factory. By tonight, we'll be nothing more than plush, silky collars on the coats of rich people."

Chapter 23

0700 hours

George felt his heart plummet to the floor. Never in his entire army career had he heard of such a cruel, inhumane practise. Certainly, he had witnessed animal cruelty and indeed, had heard many horrific stories. Charlie's story alone had shredded his heart. Sadie's death had nearly destroyed it. But this was insane. Killing all these cats merely for a human fashion statement? By Dogs' God it wasn't even that cold in England. If it were freezing then he'd understand, at least the survival component.

But even then, his thoughts harked back to Charlie in the den when he had first arrived. She had been telling the dogs that humans were a disabled, devolved, and pathetic species because they had no decent jaws, paws, noses, or fur.

She was right, he thought. If humans were the superior, highly evolved species that they claimed to be, then what need would they have of killing other species for their fur?

He felt his heart harden. A part of him began to hate humans now. He never thought he'd think like Charlie. But he saw her logic now. What right did these sick humans have to destroy the existence of other animals just because they had not thought to grow their own fur?

However, he knew he had to keep his army wits intact. If this mission was to be a success, he needed a few things organised.

Now, not only did he need to rescue over a hundred cats, but he still needed evidence regarding the murder of the old bat. Zulu's human needed freedom too, for like these cats he was innocent and stuck in a cage with no hope.

How, though, was he going to get this evidence and communicate it to humans? Yes, he could go to the police, but the abduction of cats did not prove that the monster and postie had murdered a human.

Plus, he knew he needed to ensure that the other dogs obeyed him, especially Charlie. If she knew the fate of these cats, he was not sure he could contain her rage. He needed her strong, but silent. He needed to ensure that her vengeance against the monster would be enacted.

He decided on a plan. He told the cats and reassured them that he would return, with a human and with a rescue party, before the lorry arrived. The cats were not happy about being left again, but he assured them he would return within the hour.

When he went outside, he discovered that the dogs had been listening through the door. They had heard about the cat fur trade and the plan.

They slunk back over to the fence and into the tunnel.

Chapter 24

0715 hours

His plan was to race back home immediately and return with his human. It was still dark and still cold. The sun would rise soon, so his human would be arriving home in ten minutes. "We need a human witness," he explained, "One who can testify to the police." If she brought her mobile phone and her gun, he could ensure that she not only called the police but could also protect them using her army training if needed.

The dogs were doubtful. They could not understand how he was going to communicate all this to his human. "Easy," said George, "I grab her gun, grab her mobile, and pull her towards the door. She'll recognise the urgency immediately. She trained dogs in the army to do exactly this."

"So, she'll hurry then," snapped Charlie, who continued to shiver with cold. "As will you, I hope. What about us dogs. Do we wait here? What if that Doberman shows up?"

"Just keep downwind at all times. Hide in the tunnel. That'll dull your scents. I'll need to run fast, but somehow, I'm going to have to get past that Doberman and the lake."

"Take the road, Inspector," said Sid. "I know this place. I'm sure I've been here before with my humans. If you follow the road going right, it'll lead you back to the village and the church. If you run, it'll take five minutes to get home."

As they all slunk back into the tunnel, he could hear Charlie hissing at Sid. "So, you've been here before, Sid? How come you didn't tell us? What about the Doberman?"

George grinned to himself and left them to argue.

Chapter 25

0725 hours

It wasn't quite as easy as George had hoped. First, he was flabbergasted at how unfit he'd become. He ran as fast as he could, but still had to pause to get his breath. Plus, he was worried about Zulu. Should he have gone via the lake to check on the lad's safety?

If Zulu died in the jaws of the Doberman, he doubted he could live another day. He felt a strong bond for Zulu. Like a fatherly feeling. He was proud of him too. Knowing this and knowing how dependant the lad was on him, he sprinted even faster and arrived home in enough time to witness his human staring at him in horror as he hurled himself through the dog flap.

She was standing in the kitchen, still in her nurse's dress and about to pour herself a large vodka. George meanwhile looked an absolute mess. He was covered in mud, stank of booze and fags from the old bat's house and was gasping for breath.

Her hand flew up to her mouth. "My God, George. What the hell have you been doing?"

She had little time to gather her wits. George raced past her to the bedroom, pawed open the bedside draw and grabbed her gun in his jaws. He raced back. Dropped the gun at her feet and then started dragging her backpack towards her. He knew her phone was in there, but he had no way to open the bag. Then he started barking at her and flinging his tail around frantically.

To him, the message was clear. Get your gun and bag. We've got an emergency situation to deal with.

Instead, his human did nothing. She stood there and stared at him in shock. He barked again and leaped up at her chest, staring intensely in her face.

"George. My God. What's wrong? Are you having a panic attack? Is this the PTSD? A flashback? It's okay, George. We're not in the war anymore."

He couldn't believe it. She was harking back to that psychology crap again. Had she forgotten her army training already?

He started pulling on the hem of her dress with his jaws. Pulling her to the front door. Come on, he thought. He left her at the front door, grabbed her gun from the kitchen and flung it at her feet. Then he went back for the backpack and flung that at her.

Next, he stood erect, with tail raised, facing the door and gave two warning barks. He positioned himself in the same stance he was taught in the army. The message was clear. There is a threat. They must leave now.

"What? You want me to come with you with my gun and my backpack?"

Yes, he thought. Yes, and quickly. He jumped up at her and licked her nose.

It seemed then that she got the message.

202

"Okay, George. I'll play. But if this is some joke or something that's going to be highly embarrassing, then I'm starting you on medication from the vet."

She pulled on a bulky leather jacket, put the gun in an internal pocket, 'to keep it hidden, George,' and flung on her backpack.

Chapter 26

0740 hours

They set off at a run. To follow him, she had no choice but to run. He took her back to the farmhouse via the roads, and as they grew near, he slowed the pace. He adopted a crouching stance so she could recognise his caution and adopt the same strategy. The sun had started to make a slow ascent, so they had to ensure they kept a low profile.

Slowly, they approached the tunnel. As they got near, they looked down and three little faces peered up at him. Worried faces, he thought, but also pleased to see that he had brought his human.

His human was surprised to see the dogs and initially she thought this was some rescue operation of small dogs in a tunnel. However, before she could question him further, he instructed the dogs to move through the tunnel and wait at the fence.

He pulled his human down toward the tunnel entrance. He then crawled under the tunnel and waited for her to follow.

It was clear to her that this was his intention. She stood up first and quietly surveyed the scene before her. He could see her army instincts kicking in now. He knew that she was looking for an enemy and she knew that enemy could be a human.

Quietly, she threw her backpack over the fence and then wriggled under the fence through the tunnel on her stomach. He could see her eyes. They were wide with both fear and excitement. He padded over to the other dogs who were now crouched down by the shed door.

"Any news from Zulu?" he whispered.

"Nothing," hissed Charlie. "I don't know if that's good or bad, but the Doberman hasn't returned either."

"That's gotta be good," said Rocky. "If Zulu were dead, that Doberman would be back now."

They watched in awe as his human silently treaded towards them.

"How we gonna play this?" growled Sid.

"Shhhh," hissed George, "I'll just go in first and tell the cats we are all coming in and to stay quiet."

His heart pounded rapidly like a machine gun. Everything depended on this going according to plan. His plan.

When he entered the shed, all was quiet. Quickly, he told the cats he had brought back his pack and his human. He again reiterated that they remain silent. His human and the other dogs crept into the shed.

He forgot that human vision is poor in the dark. He heard her rummaging around in her backpack. She coughed and gagged a few times and he guessed this was from the stench.

When she switched on the torch and surveyed the scene, he heard her gasp. "Oh my God, George. What the hell is this?"

A few cats meowed out sobs. Some sighed with relief. The sight of a sympathetic human gave them hope. As scene upon scene of half-starved cats and kittens lit up from the torch light, the dogs too looked on in horror. They had not seen this horrendous sight either. Not only were the cats starving and cold, many were covered in their own cat poo. Clearly the postie just left them alone to wriggle around and sleep in their own shit.

The sight of a potential rescue operation was clearly too much for these cats. Suddenly they started meowing. Loud, piercing sounds which gradually increased in frequency and intensity. George saw the danger. They were becoming hysterical. Meanwhile Elizabeth was screeching at them all to "shut up." But the rattle of the cages and the meowing of a hundred cats merely got louder.

Suddenly, George heard the front door of the house slam. Above the noise of the cats, he heard both the postie and the monster swearing and arguing as they approached the shed.

He couldn't believe it. They had got this far and now they were stuck in here about to be caught.

Quickly, he grabbed his human by the hem of her coat and dragged her towards a table blocked from view by other benches. The other dogs followed. He nudged at her to get underneath but with her size, there was no room for him. He instructed the other dogs to hide. The dogs knew the danger, but these cats, he realised, were too traumatised. Each dog found a small cubby hole or a blanket to hide under, whilst George found himself another table.

Their only hope now was that the men would do a quick check of the shed and then leave without realising that Hades was missing.

The men entered the shed and pulled a string attached to a light.

Suddenly the whole shed lit up.

Chapter 27

0800 hours

At the sight of the men entering, the cats immediately fell silent.

"Well," said the postie, "There's no one here. Nothing strange. Obviously, the little shits are just spouting off at a rat or something."

"Yeah. A rat that can open a shed door," growled the monster. "How do you explain that? You leave the door open last time you were here."

"Erm… Gee, I dunno. I doubt it. But maybe I didn't close the latch properly."

"Well, that's bloody careful of you isn't it. Anyone could've walked in," snapped the monster.

"Yeah. Doubtful though. Not out here. Not unless it's kids or some homeless type. Maybe Hades came in," said the postie. "In fact, that must be it. Hades must have come in, sniffing around and scared the cats."

"That's possible. But he was barking at something earlier on. Maybe, that something entered the shed."

"Well, there's nothing here now is there," said the postie.

"Apart from a shed full of stinking, yowling cats, it seems not. But that's not the point is it."

"What do you mean? We've got the cats. No one's here." The posties voice started to rise a few octaves. Clearly, thought George, he was nervous of the monster.

"But they could be. They could even have run off to the police by now. This stupid cat fur business of yours sucks. If anyone comes by and hears these mangey, stinking little beasts then it'll probably be jail time for both of us. I'm not going down for this shit."

"They'll be gone today," argued the Postie, "The lorry comes at 12pm. It's big money, mate. Cat fur is getting huge now. Every one of these stinking cats is worth thousands."

"It's too risky. You can't keep going out and stealing cats. We've already got a murder on our hands now. Plus, all that publicity."

George felt a stab of self-satisfied smugness. So, here it was. A possible confession. If they were referring to the murder of the old bat, then they needed to get some evidence. He hoped his human was recording it all on her mobile. He remained curled up under the table though. Nothing was certain yet.

"I don't want you carrying on this cat fur trade anymore," said the monster, "At least not on my doorstep. You wanna deal in that shit, then get a cellar like me. Now come on. Let's get some kip. I'm sick of all these disturbances."

George felt his heart sink. Was that it? That wasn't enough. They needed his human to hear more details. More information about the murder. Now it seemed they had nothing more than a mention of a murder and a shed-full of smelly cats.

As the shed light went out, a loud sound erupted from underneath one of the tables.

It was the sound of a dong. Following by the rapid fire of dings and another loud dong.

George felt his heart crash to the floor like a bomb.

It was the sound of a text on a mobile phone. His human's phone.

The light flicked back on.

Chapter 28

0815 hours

"Did you hear that?" growled the monster.

"I did." The postie sounded shocked. "Fuck me. There's someone here."

It took two seconds for them to find his human. They merely followed the sound.

George remained in his position as he listened to the sound of his human being dragged out from under the table. He was just about to charge out and attack the men when he heard his human coughing and spluttering out the words, "Stay… cough, cough… stay…" as she loudly cleared her throat and created enough noise with the struggle to hide her command.

He stayed.

Clearly, his human wanted him to remain hidden and attack later. As the men heaved his human out the door, he saw the three faces of the other dogs peering fearfully at him around various corners. He glared at them to indicate they remain hidden.

When the shed light went out and the door slammed shut, a deathly silence descended upon the shed. To everyone, it seemed, all hope was now lost. George wished he had disobeyed his human. Now, she was not only a hostage, but the men also had her mobile phone and potentially, her gun.

However, he also knew that his human was used to dealing with enemies who were in possession of guns, and that monster looked exactly the type to possess one. If it had come to a fight in the shed, then there was no way of knowing if the outcome would have been worse than the current situation.

The dogs slunk slowly out of their hiding spots and shook the dirt and fear off their fur.

Elizabeth broke the silence. In snakelike, vicious hisses she sneered at George. "So, Inspector. Your doggie plan failed. It seems we are going off to the cat factory after all. How utterly ridiculous. How stupid of us to rely on a pack of two headed dogs." She glared at George with demonic hate.

George paced slowly towards Elizabeth's cage. To everyone's shock, he stuck his face right in front of her bars and growled at her. Growled with such venom that in between the flash of his teeth, spittle's of saliva flew out his mouth, hitting Elizabeth squarely on the nose.

"I tell you now, you self-righteous, disgusting, evil little witch. If indeed we do free all the cats, I will make certain that you, and you alone, get put on that lorry and go to the fur factory. If you don't get on that lorry, then I will hunt you down and kill you myself!"

He heard a few sniggers behind him. It was not just the dogs. It was the cats as well.

Shivering, Elizabeth flattened her ears and attempted to retreat behind the big orange male.

"No good hiding behind me, gal," sniggered the fat cat. "He's got your number alright. These dogs have gone out of their way to rescue us and now you've insulted their intelligence. If he kills you, then he'll only be doing what we've all wanted to do for ages."

They heard her sob then. George felt no pity. This was the cat who had insulted Zulu. The cat who they had all been looking for. He turned to look at the other three dogs. They sat there grinning at George. He had shot down the hated Elizabeth in one foul swoop.

"So, what's the plan now," demanded the fat orange cat. "Are you gonna let us out of these cages or what?"

"No," replied George, "Unfortunately, the only way we can prove that these monstrosities have committed crimes against animals is to leave you here until my pack and I have rescued my human and called the police. Plus, we still need that damned confession. You all stay put, and you all stay silent. You got that?" he snapped, "I said, *silent!*" He knew he was angry. His plan had failed. Now they had a hostage situation to deal with. The whole thing was getting messy.

He heard a few sobs and cage rattles but reluctantly they conceded. George turned to his little renegade pack. "Well, my friends. Shall we go to the house and attack those humans or what?"

It was a command. Not a question.

Chapter 29

0830 hours

George thanked God that in the struggle, the two men had simply slammed the shed door, leaving it unhinged and therefore still open.

The dogs padded around to the back of the house. There, they found a back door with a large dog flap. Next to the dog flap was a hose and next to that, a metal chain tied to a wooden post. Clearly this was Hades' spot. George felt his heart go out to the Doberman. He glanced at Charlie who had seen the same thing. Her jaw tightened as she glared at the hose.

"Now listen," he said to the pack. "We are all going to sneak through this dog flap. I go first. When we find my human, I want you all to find yourself somewhere to hide. I do not want these men knowing we are here, okay? I need you to stay hidden and stay quiet," he glared at Charlie, "until I give the command. When I do, it is likely to be an attack command, okay? One growl. You got that?"

217

They nodded their heads furiously. Clearly, they were getting used to orders from George. He felt vindicated at last. Although the whole night had been one failed, embarrassing drama after another, at least they all seemed to respect him now.

Silently, he opened the dog flap and slid through to the other side.

Behind the dog flap was a short corridor. George waited for his pack to slip through the flap and then in single procession, they padded towards the partially opened door at the end of the corridor.

They could hear voices coming from the room. George poked his nose around the corner and realised it was a kitchen. A large kitchen. A kitchen big enough to contain yet more tables, more workbenches, and more clutter in the back area where they were about to enter.

In the front part of the kitchen, was a clearing. Through the clutter, he could see a single chair in the middle. There he saw his human. She was tied to the chair.

The postie was pacing back and forth in front of her. The monster leaned casually over a sink, watching, and smoking a cigarette.

George indicated to the three dogs to move in behind him and settle themselves into various hidden locations. He, meanwhile, took a more forward position under a small table where he could see the back of his human's chair.

Her hands were tied behind her. However, George noted that the ties were made of rope, so not the wisest move. Both he and his human were trained and experienced in hostage situations so he knew that she could, with time, untie herself. This was kid's play, for him and for her.

However, usually he was working with a trained team or as a lone dog, so there was no chance of anyone making any silly mistakes. He glanced uncertainly back at his renegade pack. He saw them all peering through various holes and gaps in the furniture. They had all seen the scene. They were all ready to fight. But the fight had to be executed at the exact time. The slightest mistake could lead to a complete failure of the whole operation. He nodded at them to indicate they remain in their positions and await his command.

George again observed his human. She was still wearing her jacket which meant she probably still had her gun in the inner pocket. He thought it unlikely that the two men had searched her. She still had on her nurse's dress, and with her yellow hair in a ponytail, and a pair of mud-stained trainers, she looked little older than a schoolgirl. If the postie recognised her from the day he had knocked on their door and asked about her fake black beard, he gave no indication.

When he had a closer look at the postie, he could see why. The man was a complete wreck. It was doubtful he could recall anything. He was still dressed in his stripy pyjamas and a dirty, old dressing gown. With his stick thin figure, he looked ridiculous. His long, thin hair hung around his face in greasy strips and his bearded face was pale and pitted with spots and small red marks. He strode back and forth erratically, flapping his arms, scratching his bum, and tugging at his beard.

The monster remained casually slumped over the sink, watching. Like a snake, thought George. The man was clearly waiting for the right moment to attack, and George believed he had every intention to kill if not torture his human. The monster looked on, with an amused expression on his face.

"So," challenged the postie, pointing an accusing, yet trembling, thin finger at George's human, "You say you were just out looking for your dog and happened to accidently enter our premises and go and look in our shed?"

219

"Well, yes. Absolutely," replied his human. "I was just walking past your house, and I thought I heard a bark in the shed." She shrugged. "I didn't want to knock on your door so early, so I just ran in quickly to check."

George felt his ears burn with pride. His human spoke in clear, calm tones and lied through her teeth with ease. If she had her senses about her, she would already know that George was watching and waiting for her command. He saw her lift one finger up. It meant 'wait'.

However, he also knew that showing too much confidence in such an unusual, and dangerous situation would appear suspicious. She was a hostage and so far, no one had mentioned her army career.

She seemed to sense this too. When she spoke again it was in nervous tones, which he knew were feigned. "However, when I entered the shed, it was so dark, I could barely see a thing. Then when I heard your voices, I got scared and hid under a table. Luckily, I had my small torch so I could see the table."

Boy she was clever, thought George. She wasn't even going to admit she'd seen the cats.

"So," said the postie in dramatic, albeit raspy tones, "You were hiding under the table when myself and my dear friend here," he indicated the monster by flinging out a skinny arm, "were having a discussion about our plans, with," he emphasized, "the shed light on." He smiled thinly and leaned in closer towards the woman's face.

"Well, yes," she said, "I guess. But I was so scared of getting caught, that I couldn't focus on what you were saying. I'm just worried about my dog." Again, more feigned, nervous tones.

George felt his heart plummet. His human had failed. Now, by denying already that she had heard anything, she had practically admitted to hearing it all.

Too overdone, he thought. The less said, the better.

"So," said the postie, now pacing back and forth in a more strident fashion, "What your saying is that you saw nothing, heard nothing and as a result, know nothing? Am I correct?" He turned towards her and sneered. He knew she had heard everything.

"Well, yeah. I mean... I really don't want any trouble. I'm a nurse. I just want to find my dog and go home to bed."

"Right," nodded the postie, whilst tugging at his beard. "Keep your job. Right. Well, I can tell you now, Missie," his voice raised in volume, "That you won't be keeping any job if you go blabbing to the police!" He was becoming more animated. More volatile. Unpredictable. George knew the monster would have to step in soon.

Her index finger remained single, straight, and upright. Still no attack, thought George. In-between finger signs, she was gradually tugging at the rope but had still to untie it. She must be waiting for free hands he decided. Then she could use her gun. If he snuck out and attempted to untie the rope, he would be seen. They had to remain in position. Not only that, but they still hadn't got a full confession.

It was then, that the monster stood up and paced slowly towards her. "So," he said, in thoughtful, quiet tones, "You say no one knows you're here, eh? Well let's just check your mobile phone then. See if you've made any calls whilst you were in that shed."

He had her phone in his hands. "Mmmm....no 999 calls to the police then. But what's this? An unread text received at eight fifteen this morning. That'd be about the same time as we caught you in our shed, right?" He scratched the black stubble on his beard, as if highly puzzled.

What a pair of drama queens, thought George. It seemed they had to drag out this whole hostage situation like some silly scene in the movies.

"Ah," said the monster, suddenly smiling. "It seems to be from one of your work friends. Someone called Margie?"

"Oh yeah. I worked with her last night," confirmed his human.

"And it says something about alcohol. Alcohol on your breath."

"Oh really? Seriously? What does it say?" George's human arched her back in surprise.

Ah, clever, thought George. Change the topic. Delay the scene so she could work on her rope.

"It says, 'Heads up, Penny. Management smelt alcohol on your breath last night. They want to call you in for a meeting. They just asked me about it. Don't worry. I kept quiet. Deny everything, and don't forget to join that dating agency. You probably just drink 'cause you're lonely. I still think you should get a lodger'. Mmm."

The Monster started pacing, whilst staring at the phone. "Well," he turned to the postie, "It looks like we've got an alcoholic nurse, whose no doubt neurotic, and who lives alone with her missing dog. A young, pretty nurse who heard and saw everything in our shed. What do you think we should do with that information?"

The postie stared at the monster. In shock, thought George. The man was starting to see where this was leading.

Damn, thought George. The disappearance or murder of an alcoholic, neurotic nurse, and single too, would be an easy crime to cover up. What the hell was up with her. Drinking at work? Jeez. He'd have to get her off that stuff if they ever got out of this situation. Christ, if she lost her job, they'd be homeless too. What a mess, he thought. Maybe he should just ignore her finger and get on with the business of rescuing her and killing that monster.

But then he realised that was exactly what she was trying to prevent. If he killed the monster, then the whole thing would lead to one big mess. Potentially, the death of everyone. He really needed that confession. At this rate they were never going to get it.

Penny intervened. "Well, it's a shit job, isn't it? I mean who wouldn't go into work half cut? How else am I supposed to earn a wage whilst coping with all that stench and death?"

Changing the topic again, smiled George. Another clever tactic. A tactic to gain empathy and time from the enemy, or to even look somewhat rebellious and therefore more akin to the enemy rather than her job.

The postie looked horrified. In fact, thought George he looked downright angry. He started shaking his fist at her. "Are you telling me that you, a nurse, working for the taxpayer, paid with taxes that I pay, are going into work half drunk? What if I was your patient, eh? What if you made some horrible error and caused my death?" He was yelling now.

George choked down a snigger. This. Coming from a drug-dealing postie who probably had no regard for taxes. A postie, he suspected, who was undoubtably highly addicted to amphetamines.

"Well, I doubt anyone is going to care if she goes missing then really, eh," continued the monster. "Looks like she's fairly dispensable. I mean, why let her go back to work if she's just gonna put all those patients in danger, eh? Managers will probably just give her a warning, and she's going to deny it anyway."

The monster stared at the postie. They both turned to look at Penny.

"Do you know what?" The monster grinned. "I think we'll keep her. Yep. Stick her in the cellar for a while. Our little playmate, eh?" He shrugged. "I mean you said so yourself. She's seen everything, heard everything and so obviously," he turned towards Penny and raised his voice, "She knows everything!"

Suddenly he flung his arm across his chest and back handed Penny across her face.

Penny remained staunchly silent. No yells. No tears. No pleas for mercy. George felt proud. But also, impatient. She was still struggling with the rope whilst keeping her finger up.

The postie started pacing around in circles frantically. "But if we lock her in the cellar, then what about when the coppers come around. I mean, she'll be missing. They'll get out the sniffer dogs and search the woods. What if they sniff her trail right back to us?"

The monster looked thoughtful. It was a good point, thought George. However, George knew that he was not going to let her go. "It's too late for that now. You clear out those cats and clean up their shit today, okay. The sniffer dogs might track her here, but they won't trace her down in the cellar. It's a bloody fortress down there. We'll rake up the dirt outside and mop the kitchen."

The postie looked doubtful. "What do we say to the cops, then?"

"Easy. We just say we were sleeping in our beds when we heard Hades' barking. We got up, had a look around for an intruder, found nothing, so returned to bed. If those sniffer dogs smell her around here, they'll just have to assume she was trespassing. Looking for her dog. I might send a text to Marge from Penny here and tell her that our little lassie is out searching for her dog. Done. See? Perfect." He slung her mobile onto the kitchen bench.

The postie started pacing back and forth again. "But we can't have the cops crawling all over the place straight after that murder. It's too soon. Why did you have to go and kill that old woman? I don't want any involvement in all this. Now you're talking about abducting a human."

The monster turned to the postie. "Well now you've gone and brought that up, right in front of our hostage here, what do you

224

expect me to do? Now, she not only knows about the murder, but she knows exactly who was killed and by whom!" He slammed his fist onto the kitchen bench. The postie jumped and clutched his chest. "You're a bloody loose cannon. Can't you ever keep your trap shut?"

The monster walked towards the postie and pushed his fist in his face. "Don't think you're innocent in all this. You've pretty much ensured that this lassie here, this little nurse, isn't ever gonna be leaving my cellar alive!"

The postie's eyes grew wide with horror. George felt his heart hammering away in his chest.

"If you hadn't abducted that cat, then none of this would have happened. No murder. No hostage," continued the monster.

The postie started stuttering. "W... what do you mean? How can you justify all that just because of a cat abduction?" he was still bouncing from one foot to the other. The monster walked away and lit up a cigarette.

"Your bloody cat fur business was interfering with mine, wasn't it. You go and steal that old woman's cat and she makes a massive fuss. There were too many eyes in the street. How can I get on with business if everyone's peeking through their curtains all day?"

"Yeah, but that's all it would have been. Just neighbours getting paranoid about a cop murdering a cat. You could have let it go."

"True," said the monster, "But the opportunity to get rid of that cop was too good. All those neighbours baying for his blood and him living right opposite my drug dealers. If that cop had gotten suspicious, I would have lost my deal with them. That's big bucks."

"So actually, it was bloody convenient then wasn't it. I abducted the cat. You killed the old woman; the cop got the blame and now I doubt he'll ever get free. If he does, I doubt he'll wanna live with neighbours who think he's a terrorist. Those fake terrorist rumours and those death threats we started were brilliant." The postie laughed nervously. Clearly, thought George, the postie was trying to re-establish some kinship with the monster and calm him down.

"True," the monster agreed. "So, stop getting paranoid. The cop's in jail. It was damn lucky one of the dealers stayed home and heard the cop running down the street after cutting off his beard too. You planted some of his beard in the dead woman's house and the cop's dog has done a runner. I put the blood on the cop's doorstep and the dealers said they saw a man with a black beard and a black dog leave the old woman's house. There is nothing to link either you or me to the murder now. You were just the poor, innocent postie who found her."

The postie stiffened. "But hang on. What about the gun?"The monster shrugged. "Easy," he said, "Tonight, I'm gonna sling the gun over his back fence. The sniffer dogs are out tomorrow. They'll find it in the bushes." The monster slapped his hand on the posties back.

Then he laughed. "You've got to admit it mate. We've tied the whole thing up like a leg-a-lamb. Now," he said, turning to Penny, "We've just got to deal with this little problem. Lucky I've got a cellar, eh." He grinned triumphantly and winked at her. Then he slapped her around the face again.

Despite the slap, George felt his heart soar. Finally, at last, they had the whole sordid confession. Heard by his human. Now all they had to do was free her and Zulu could have his human back.

He noted that Penny had nearly untied her rope. She was near to escape. However, he had been so engrossed in the proceedings, that he had forgotten to monitor his little pack.

Unbeknown to him, Charlie had been becoming increasingly agitated. He turned to look at her, but it was too late. Her rage erupted like a volcano. Without looking at George, she flew past him and ran straight to the ankles of the monster.

Chapter 30

0915 hours

Her attack was so sudden, so fast, so frenzied, that all anyone could do was look on in shock. This was something no one had expected, least of all the postie. He stared on in horror, and then burst out laughing. The monster lurched around the kitchen jumping frantically from one foot to the other. He screamed out in pain as Charlie ripped his trousers and drove her teeth into his ankles.

As he scuttled around the kitchen, two more shocking things happened. The first was that the monster suddenly got his act together and kicked Charlie across the kitchen. As she slid over to a corner, her eyes met George. She was winded and clearly in pain. However, her eyes gleamed with killer pleasure.

In that same moment, two black shapes streaked past George. Hades and Zulu. Hades immediately launched himself at the monster and dragged him to the floor by his collar. The monster was immobilized and clearly terrified, as Hades' salivating jaws growled and snapped at his face.

Zulu went straight for the postie. In the same vein as Charlie, he tore at the postie's pyjama bottoms. Because the postie was so skinny, his pyjamas quickly slipped down to his ankles. Suddenly he was lurching around trying to protect not just his ankles, but his bare bum and privates. As the postie tripped and fell, Rocky and Sid rushed past. They too started snapping and biting at the two men, Sid on the monster, Rocky on the postie.

George looked on with pride. He glanced over at Charlie. Before he could consider the pain in her eyes, he acted. He raced over to his human, undid the rest of her rope, and then immediately charged straight towards the throat of the postie.

As he glared down into the petrified face of the snivelling man, he realised the irony. He was snarling and raging over a white man, with a white beard. There was no black-bearded enemy at all.

Standing beside him, snarling, and snapping at various bits of the postie was Zulu. A proud and loyal soldier. A true and great friend. Then he laughed. Rocky was busy rummaging around and sniffing at the postie's privates, causing the postie to shriek into the jaws of George's salivating teeth.

In that time, Penny had managed to free herself from her chair. She raced over to the kitchen sideboard, grabbed her phone, and made an emergency call to report an ongoing hostage situation. After that, she grabbed her gun, took off the safety, and pointed it squarely at the head of the monster.

George looked over at Charlie. She was getting slowly up onto her paws. She limped over towards the monster. She was clearly in pain, thought George. But God she was such a determined little dog. Nothing would stop her having the last bark. Or growl.

As he continued to salivate and growl at the postie, he watched her.

He saw her peer over, and stare deeply into the eyes of the monster. So, he could remember her, concluded George, who seemed to be now watching the scene in slow motion.

The monster looked up at her. He had Hades snapping away in his face, a gun at his head and now this fiery little Foxie who had first attacked him, staring at him with those eyes. Eyes, thought George, one could never forget. Eyes of pain; eyes of trauma; eyes of rage and hate.

The monster stared back at her. Suddenly he choked out, "Charlie? My God. Is that really you?"

Then she snarled. Snarled with all the venom she could muster. The rage and hate leached through her. Despite her size, to George she looked like a huge, noble wolf in the wild as she stood triumphantly over her prey.

Then suddenly, with one rapid movement, she grabbed hold of the monster's nose with her jaws and pulled. Pulled so hard, that with a blood curling scream from the monster, it came right off. She turned and slung it into the corner. The same one where he had kicked her earlier.

With her front paws now standing on his head, she raised her head and howled. Howled with all the victory, all the triumph and all the emotion she could express in one full howl.

It was both chilling and thrilling. George felt his heart expand with pride.

Before he could muster up any more emotion, the police arrived.

Chapter 31

0930 hours

It was a shocking scene. One the police had no doubt never encountered before. Two men, one half-naked, were lying on the floor. Six dogs stood snarling and snapping at them whilst a young female wearing a nurse's dress stood squarely over the monster, pointing her gun at him.

Initially, they expressed surprise. They had expected the female to be held hostage. Instead, it was the two males. The police were entirely confused by it all. Luckily, George's human was able to quickly explain.

As the dogs stood over their enemy, she took them over to a table, sat two of them down, and explained the whole story. Right down to the abduction of Elizabeth, the fur trade business, the drug dealing, the murder of the old bat with the fake clues, the abduction of herself, and the rescue operation, which had been led by the pack of dogs. To prove it, she let them listen to the confession she had recorded on her mobile phone. She had set it on record in the shed and let it run throughout the whole sordid confession in the kitchen.

The first cop's face flushed with anger. "Are you telling me one of our lot is stuck in a cell accused of a murder these two snivelling cowards committed?" he asked.

The second cop added, "Yeah. That'll be Peter Harrison. He's one of us. A great bloke he is. Been through bloody hell over this business."

George noticed Zulu homing in on their conversation. When Zulu looked back at him, he said, "Well done, Son. Well done."

And Zulu. How proud he looked. How victorious. Finally, they had freed his human, and it was all down to the strength, determination, and loyalty of this young, small dog.

George loved the lad. He loved Charlie too. Yet after the war, after Sadie, he thought he would never find it in his heart to love another dog again.

How glad he was that he had taken the plunge, listened to his gut, and flown out the dog flap earlier that night. He had gained so much. They all had.

Suddenly, Hades left the neck of the monster. A monster who was now lying there, in a state of paralytic fear.

The police were swift. They stood up and pointed their tasers at Hades. Neither it seemed wanted to risk being victimised by a dog who had yet to prove his innocence.

However, Hades merely padded calmly over to the edge of the rug in the kitchen. He began pawing at it. It was clear he wanted it removed. One cop plucked up enough courage to help Hades pull it to one side.

There, underneath, was a trap door. When the copper opened it and went down the stairs, they heard, "Bloody hell, Simon. There's a meth lab the size of a factory down here." Then, "Shit. Look at all these guns!"

George wagged his tail victoriously. He noticed the other dogs were all wagging their tails and wriggling their bums in pleasure. He raced up to Penny, jumped up to face her and planted a huge wet kiss on her nose. Now the police could lock away these monstrosities forever.

Which they did and Zulu's human came home.

Epilogue

Whilst Charlie recovered from her broken ribs, Zulu's human, Peter, had become very friendly with Penny. George suspected that some sort of romance was blossoming. His human was changing for the better. She drank less alcohol for starters. Watched less crime documentaries and seemed to be eating a healthier diet. George felt relieved. He had been getting sick of the vindaloos she'd been eating, in order, she said, "to help you with your fear of spicey food smells, George."

The beards disappeared as well. Although that was probably because he now went out for walks with her. He still kept guard though. He wasn't stupid.

Zulu and Hades visited too. Hades had been adopted by Zulu's human, who thought that the name Hades, meaning Hell, was far to cruel a name to give to a 'four-legged-hero'. Zulu pranced about and wiggled his tail with glee. "He's renamed him Nelson, Inspector. After Nelson Mandala, the famous African peacemaker."

Nelson chortled. George knew that Nelson was struggling with the idea of cosy, happy families, and warm, comfy sofas. He had told George that he kept expecting the hose. George had reassured him, "You are simply suffering from Post-traumatic Disorder, my friend. Perhaps, my human can help you?" Then he had burst out laughing as he explained to Nelson the horrific details of his own psychological therapies and the hateful fake black beard.

"By Dogs' God Inspector," growled Nelson, "That sounds worse than the hose? Are your sure your human is good enough for Zulu's human here?"

They all glanced at the two humans who were gossiping and laughing as they sipped at a glass of their chosen poison. Penny, vodka. Peter, rum.

Zulu sighed. "They make such a lovely couple. I hope they marry."

From those conversations, the dogs had also learned of the fate of the monster and the postie. Both had been sent to prison for multiple crimes. The monster had admitted that he had shot the old woman, then slit her throat open with a knife. He had forced Nelson to sink his jaws into the wound to make it look like a dog was the culprit. For Nelson, that meant he was not considered a dangerous dog and he was able to live with Zulu.

As for Charlie, she was never implicated in the crime of a nose amputation. Penny had informed the police of how Charlie had defended her and then had her ribs broken by the monster.

Sid moved in with Rocky. His hooligan humans had been arrested on drug charges and the police suspected that Sid had been suffering from neglect. Shortly after that, Sid's appearance radically changed. The shaggy mass of hair on his head had been cut into a shorter, more stylish look and his groomed white fur gleamed in the sunlight. He had evidently been bathed in lavender shampoo.

Furthermore, it now looked like someone had attempted a rather poor job of thinning out his tail whilst adding an odd shaped little pom-pom on the end. He had also gained weight. The whole affect made him appear like a completely different dog. Indeed, he even seemed more relaxed and amenable. He avoided eye-contact with George though. He was probably ashamed of his past behaviour, thought George. Either that, or now with his new appearance, he didn't feel he presented a tough enough exterior to pose any real threat.

Some of the cats had been sent to a local cat shelter but many were sent back to their original humans. With all the publicity, the ones in the shelter were certain to find caring companions to adopt them. No one ever heard about Elizabeth. No one wanted to. Zulu kept harking on about seeing her hiding out in various locations, but the others were doubtful. George suspected the lad was paranoid. His enemy had simply disappeared and no doubt this made Zulu somewhat anxious.

They had all been big news in the media for a while. Photos taken. Front page news. TV interviews – for the humans anyway. It was quite draining for George. A horribly public affair. All that time he'd spent trying to keep a low profile and suddenly he and his renegade pack were public heroes. In fact, the whole village got involved. It seemed they had suddenly forgotten how they had been implicated in the attack on Zulu and his human. Now, they wanted to sell their stories. To George's amazement, it suddenly appeared that all along, both he and Zulu had been everyone's best friend. For ages!

He was proud though. Dog stories and Dog heroes were the talk of the country. It was validation, thought George. Recognition, of what all dogs do, and all dogs can do.

***

239

That night he snuck out to the dog den to meet the others. It had been ages since he had seen Charlie, so he was keen to go.

Zulu told them all about what happened after he had left them at the fence. "It was madness," said Zulu as he paced around the others at a dizzying rate. "I can't believe I agreed to it now."

Nelson sat back, grinning away like an embarrassed arsehole.

"So yeah," continued Zulu, "I don't think I've ever run as fast or as long in my life. By the time I got to the lake I was knackered. But I swam anyway. It was like swimming through sludge."

Ever the talker, thought George as he grinned away to himself.

Zulu told them how he had arrived at the statue, crawled onto the platform in a pathetic heap and lay there thinking he was going to die.

"But when I looked across the lake, I saw Hades, er, I mean Nelson. He looked so angry, but he was terrified of the water, weren't you, Nelson. You refused to swim?

"It was the perfect plan," continued Zulu, ignoring Nelson's embarrassed face. "After that, it was pretty easy, well, I mean," he glanced at Nelson, who was starting to look annoyed, "It wasn't that easy. First, I had to get through all the anger Hades, I mean Nelson had. That took a bit of a while, but better for you guys I guess." He shrugged casually.

Charlie was sitting on her crate. Re-establishing dominance no doubt, thought George. "So, you too have been exposed to water torture," she challenged, her anger ever present.

Nelson flattened his ears and stared at the muddy floor. "Yes," he mumbled. "But it was just the hose mainly. Enough times to make me fear water though."

Charlie's eyes softened. George realised he had never actually witnessed her truly sympathize with anyone before. But before he could take a snapshot of this scene and save it to memory, Zulu started yapping on again.

"Inspector, did you know about the previous owner of the farmhouse? The man who owned it before the monster."

George shook his head. To his surprise, Zulu burst out laughing. "Sir," he gasped, in between chortles, "I can't believe your human hasn't told you."

"Told me what, Zulu," snapped George. He felt his ears burn. What had his human kept from him now?

"Sir, the house was previously owned by a secret arms dealer. A double agent. Apparently, he was selling arms to the insurgents in the war. Even the Taliban apparently. All kinds of evidence was found in the basement. Logbooks and guns. They've arrested him now. Today, I think."

"And?" quizzed George impatiently. "What's this got to do with me?"

Zulu scratched his ears. He looked awkward for a moment. But still, ever the one to love a story, he continued, "Sir. The man they arrested is a Colonel in the army. A man named Colonel George Penkins."

Yet again, George felt his heart plummet to the ground. In fact, it fell further than that. It fell right into the muddy ground and joined up with all the dead soldiers and all his dog friends who had died in that war. It lay buried there, suffocating and drowning in a dirty grave.

Suddenly, he heard another laugh. He looked up from the floor and saw Charlie. She was rolling about on her side on her crate, clutching in pain at her ribs, and laughing hysterically.

George felt his wounded heart harden. He growled loudly, which stopped her in her tracks.

"Oh, Inspector," she giggled, as she tried to recover herself. "I'm sorry. Truly I am. It really does seem like your life has been plagued by a vast array of little red herrings."

She had to rub his nose in it, he thought angrily. Always. Always. She seemed to want to see his delusions shattered. Watch his ego fragment yet again.

So, he left. He trotted off, then began to run. He ran for so long that when he finally arrived at the cemetery and the annoyingly squeaky gate, he collapsed on a grave and reconsidered life and the best options for death.

As he lay there, staring sadly up at the new crescent moon, he felt a warm little body beside him. It was Charlie.

"Does it give you pleasure, Charlie?" he asked quietly.

"Does what, Inspector?"

"This constant denigration of me. This need you seem to have to pull me to pieces. To put Zulu down. To put us all down."

There was silence as Charlie contemplated this.

Then she spoke, in her ever-arrogant tones, "If you mean, Inspector, does it give me pleasure to rip apart the veil of illusion and reveal to a being the truth of all matters, then yes. It does."

"So, you enjoy making others feel miserable then?" he asked glumly.

"No. It's not like that at all, George." He noticed that for the first time she used his name. "To me, misery is living a life in which you do not know the truth of it all and therefore the truth of yourself. For me, living a lie makes you weak. It leaves the door open for others to come in and abuse their power. So, does it give me pleasure?" she asked, "Well no. Not unless you do something about it."

"What do you mean now, Charlie?" He sighed. He was still laying on the grave staring up at the moon.

242

"Well," she chomped, "If you go back to your warm comfy sofa and live a life slumped on it doing nothing, then no. It won't give me pleasure. But if you completely ditch your fears and spread the word, then yes, I will be glad."

"And what of Zulu? You would have destroyed that lad with your bullying. Destroyed his mind and spirit."

"Ah yes," sighed Charlie. "I'm afraid you have a point there, Inspector. Much as I hate to admit it. But yes. We would have destroyed the very thing that gives us all strength. Something I had never considered until tonight."

"Which is?" George asked.

"Love, Inspector. Of us all, Zulu is the only one who truly feels and is empowered by love. I think perhaps myself and my little pack were a tad jealous of that."

"You think?" George sat up. Was she serious? "You think?" he repeated. "Well tell me, Charlie. Now you know this, is there any room in your own heart for love?"

She coughed and scratched an ear. At last, he thought. He had finally made her feel uneasy.

George sat up and stared into her brandy eyes. "Do you still hate every human, Charlie? Even if they're not power-hungry-red herrings and human monsters?"

Again, she scratched her ears and stared silently at the mouldy gravestone beside him. Then she looked up and sighed. "Yes, Inspector. I do hate them. I hate them all. I don't know if I can ever forgive or forget. Even the nice humans, who are perhaps ignorant but probably out of choice, drive me insane with their own selfish need for greed and control."

"Perhaps if your first human – that murdering monster – had been nicer, then you would not hold such intense beliefs, Charlie?" he suggested.

"Perhaps," she replied quietly.

"I've got an idea, Charlie," he said, "Come with me."

They trotted through the graveyard, through the woods and over the bridge towards the marble white soldiers glimmering on the lake.

"You see those statues over there on the lake?" said George.

She stared intensely at the soldiers. "Yes. War soldiers yet not one war dog amongst them. Typical," she snapped, "They throw you into the war to risk death to save them and for what? Power and greed again, Inspector. What's your point?"

"That life isn't fair, Charlie. There is both good and bad in all of us. But we can't let it eat away at us. If you do, then the humans have won. That hate will destroy you. Yet it is a hate that is ultimately fuelled by fear. You are the most courageous little dog I have ever met, yet you are only seeing the world through one aspect. That of hate. Unless you battle through your own fear, that hate will destroy you."

"I'm still alive aren't I," she countered.

"Not quite, Charlie. Yes, you have survived. But are you genuinely happy? Are you ever at peace? To learn my lessons, I had to crash through my dog flap, battle through shame, anger, fear, and hatred. I had to let go of all my dearly held beliefs. I see a new world now. One of hope. Regardless of my original owner, I feel truly at peace."

Charlie's eyes darkened and she raised her tail. "Your point, Inspector. Just get to it, please."

"My point is this, Charlie." Suddenly he lunged towards her, grabbed her by the scruff of her neck and flung her out, as far as he could, into the still, dark lake.

George glided up to her thrashing body as she sank, then rose, spluttered for air, then sank again.

"Swim, Charlie," he said gently in her ears, as she struggled up again. "Swim."

244

Then suddenly she swam.

Right next to him.

Towards the statue.

Gracefully.

Calmly.

As all dogs can, and all dogs should.

When finally, she stepped up onto the statue and shook her fur, she howled. Howled right up into the shiny new moon. Howled and howled like a wolf in the wild. Yet it was not mournful or pleading.

It was the howl of victory.

A howl that called the other dogs. The dogs who all, including Nelson, jumped into the lake, and swam swiftly towards the statue.

When finally, Charlie stopped howling, she glared triumphantly into the eyes of George. She had done it. She had overcome her fear.

As the other dogs joined them on the statue, they all grinned.

They were there. Standing on that statue.

Standing next to the war soldiers, as testament to the bravery of all dogs. They all looked up at the moon, and it was then, just then, that the moon smiled back.

Meet The Author

Lee Huggett has a degree in psychology, has studied English literature, and has worked as a mental health nurse for 22 years.

She has a keen sense of justice and a natural desire to protect the underdog. She has always thought outside the box and consequently, she is never able to believe the conventional narrative of the establishment.

Lee Huggett was born and bred in England. She spent part of her childhood in South Africa during apartheid and now lives in Australia with her beloved dogs, Penny and Zulu.

This is her first novel.

www.ingramcontent.com/pod-product-compliance
Lightning Source LLC
Chambersburg PA
CBHW020401120726
47904CB00002B/652